No Hero for the Kaiser

BY RUDOLF FRANK

TRANSLATED FROM THE GERMAN BY
PATRICIA CRAMPTON

ILLUSTRATIONS BY KLAUS STEFFENS

LOTHROP, LEE & SHEPARD BOOKS ♦ NEW YORK

Library of Congress Cataloging in Publication Data: Frank, Rudolf.   No hero for the kaiser.   Translation of: Der Junge, der seinen Geburtstag vergass.   Summary: Jan, a fourteen-year-old Polish boy whose town is invaded in World War I, joins a German battalion and experiences the horrors of battle. 1. World War, 1914–1918—Juvenile fiction. [1. World War, 1914–1918—Fiction] I Title.   PZ7.F8516No   1986   [Fic] 85-23989   ISBN 0-688-06093-5

Book design by Sylvia Frezzolini

❖ A BOY WHO FORGOT HIS BIRTHDAY

H E WAS FOURTEEN YEARS OLD TODAY: FOUR-
teen years old on September 14, 1914. That
should have been easy to remember, but he
had forgotten. It was already three o'clock in the afternoon, and Jan had not even thought of it one single
time. How could a boy forget his birthday? Impossible,
surely, if things are as they should be.

In fact, nothing was as it should be on this day when
the world closed in on Jan, with hideous noise and
fearsome chaos and destruction. Kopchovka, a Polish
hamlet surrounded by slender poplar trees, was barely
recognizable. On the far side, on the heights, among the
potato and turnip fields, lay the Russian soldiers who
had stormed through the village the day before, shouting and cursing, with their guns and cannon. On the
other side of the village behind the wood were the Germans, at whom their curses had been aimed.

The Russians would really have preferred to stay in
Kopchovka. There was an inn there, and there were
spirits, fowl, and pork. But while they were still
carousing in the taproom, on the village street, and in

1

the houses and stables, the distant thud of cannon came closer, like a thunderstorm brewing. And as if the storm had already broken, women, boys, girls, and soldiers began to rush around in confusion; trumpets sounded, and suddenly the Russians had swept out of the village like the wind. Now they were firing down from the low hills into the village. It sounded like the high-pitched whine of mosquitoes as they fly past your ear looking for a place to settle and bite: zzzzzz — a thin, sharp noise, full of sly malice. Jan knew that any one of those invisible whining bullets could kill man or beast on the spot. A dreadful feeling! But there was worse to come. The heavy shells began to howl noisily through the air. Jan was a brave boy. He had never known fear, not even when he had had to pass alone through the forests of Vielki in the pitch-dark night, but fear seized him now. For now it came from the other side as well, over there where the Germans were. They must believe that the Russians were still in Kopchovka, and they fired and fired. . . . Jan closed his eyes and ducked his head. It was as if the devilish thing now rushing straight at him were going to fall right between his own shoulder blades. *Crash!* In front of him the earth spurted up, thick, black as if it were from hell itself, spurting high, even higher than Panie Ostrovsky's barn, and dealt him a blow that knocked him over backward. When he tried to get up again, he was covered with muck, and the beautiful tree laden with ripe plums was gone — simply vanished. In its place was a deep, sinister hole.

Jan had often looked longingly at that tree in autumn

when its boughs were heavy with sweet, deep-purple fruit. Once — no twice, really, he had climbed stealthily into its branches. But the second time when he landed at the bottom he had been beaten with a thick stick until his back was as blue as the forbidden fruit. Fat Ostrovsky was the *panie*, and *panie* means master! Panie Ostrovsky was a stern and bad-tempered master, but now an invisible horror had snatched away the whole beautiful tree with all its plums and no *panie* was running out with a stick, cursing; there was no one at all, just the ever-worsening whistling across streets and farmyards, the hissing and howling above the rooftops. Then — another of the gigantic things: *boommmm*, it fell straight into the barn. Jan ran away and plunged into the ditch at the side of the road. A frightened backward glance showed thick, white smoke billowing from the barn and a little red flame flitting along the roof — like a tightrope dancer. This year's harvest was in that barn, so how would they bake bread now, Jan wondered. The flame grew larger and larger. Surely something must be done! But no one came to put it out; there was not a soul to be seen anywhere. Jan thought of his father, who would surely have helped, but his father was away at the war, fighting for the Russian emperor, the Little Father Tsar, as they used to say. Perhaps he too was firing at that very moment into some village where a boy lay in a ditch, afraid.

Jan had been very sad when his father had left a month before. That Little Father Tsar could not be a kind little father, taking a poor boy's own little father away! What were the tsar and the Russians to him? He and his father spoke German — half the village spoke German, and the rest were Poles and spoke Polish. His dear father! How sad he had been when he kissed Jan good-bye. And Uncle Peter, who had promised to take care of Jan, was very different from his father and did nothing but sit in the inn getting drunk, leaving him to look after himself.

"Uncle Peter! Uncle Peter!" he shouted. In this dreadful solitude he would have been glad even of his drunken uncle. But no Uncle Peter came, only the constant rush and roar of the shells: the Russians' from the right, the Germans' from the left. There was no difference.

But suddenly he spotted another living thing: there on the dung heap snuffled grocer Kaczmar's big sow. They must have forgotten to slaughter it. Why did the animal suddenly scream so horribly? It screamed like a human being, and now it was running on three legs as if the devil were after it, moaning dreadfully and squealing, through the apple trees, around and around in circles, with terror in its eyes. Its right hind leg was bloody and dragging. A bullet had done it, one of those malicious mosquitoes with their angry, high-pitched buzzing. What if the same thing happened to him as had happened to the poor pig? He had only two legs, so he would not even be able to run away — he would have to lie there, dying of thirst and hunger, bleeding to death. Hunger! It was only then that he noticed how desperately hungry he was. He had eaten nothing since the evening before. And thirst! That was even

more painful, unbearable. Uncle Peter, he thought.
No matter what, I must get to Uncle Peter.

The house lay on the other side of the village street,
low-built, grey and dirty, the windowpanes broken, the
roof falling in, and a door hanging loose. His uncle had
let everything go, and normally Jan would have been
quite happy never to see that house again. But now he
longed for it. It was his only refuge. There might even
be a swallow of milk there. And even if there was no
milk, there was the well in the yard behind the house.
The Russians had not taken that away. With quick re-
solve the boy jumped out of the ditch in which he had
lain until now and was about to run across, when
boommmm! Another explosion, just in front of his
uncle's house, split the ground with a dreadful tearing
sound.

Jan felt as if a giant had struck him in the chest with
his fist. The ground went from under him, he flew
backward and cracked against the wall. He lay there.
His whole body ached. He was deafened. He saw his
uncle's house through a mist. Had the walls become
transparent? He could see the big, fat stove on which
he had been sleeping in recent weeks, saw the picture
of the Holy Virgin on the left-hand wall, but the back
wall — good God! He could see the well in the yard
behind — the well from which he had been going to
drink. The back wall had gone and half the roof with it.
The house was finished.

"Uncle Peter!" Jan shouted. "What shall we do
now?" But there was no answer. All he could hear was

the dreadful squealing of the wounded pig as it hobbled down the village street and disappeared behind Panie Ostrovsky's farmhouse.

Jan looked about him. The wall he had been thrown against in the blast was the wall of the inn. Perhaps his uncle was in there, or the landlady? She liked him. Maybe she would give him a bit of bread, perhaps even a glass of milk. After all, she had given him a red-dyed egg at Easter.

"Mrs. Goloborotka!" he shouted, opening the door to the taproom. "Matka! . . . Goloborotka!" But there was no sign of the fat, red-faced landlady who usually smiled across the counter at him. The room was as empty as the rest of the village. There was nothing but a desolate rubble of broken glass and bottles and over-turned chairs. Fat, black flies crawled across the dirty tabletops, feasting on pools of spilled spirits.

They've left me on my own, thought Jan, all alone in the village. No one remembered me. Despite his brave-ness, he began to feel utterly wretched. To be so en-tirely alone is worse than a beating. He cried out aloud, cried out as he never had in his life before.

Ssshshsh — *boommmm!* Outside there was another thundering crash, like an answer to his shouts, a com-mand: Ssshshsh, be silent! Frightened to death, Jan was silent. He thought suddenly of God — had He too abandoned him in the midst of this dreadful battering, caught between Russian and German rifles and can-non?

"Dear God, oh, dear God, what's going to happen to me? Where's my uncle, where's Mrs. Goloborotka?

Dear God, tell me what to do, where to go. Our Father, who art in heaven, the soldiers said the Germans nail all the children to barn doors. Thy kingdom come, I'm so thirsty! Give us this day our daily bread, just a little bit of it — " Hark! What was that? It came from outside, but it was not the appalling rush and roar — it sounded like footsteps: taptap — taptap — "Mrs. Goloborotka?" No, it was like the footsteps of a child or a —

"Bow-wow-wow-wow-wow!" he heard. "Bow-wow-wow-wow-wow," as Jan leaped at the dog, clutched it around the neck, and hugged it to him, a filthy bundle of fur, but with two faithful eyes, and a red, lolling tongue licking his cheeks, ears, and hands.

"Flox! Flox! Flox!" cried Jan, "Floxie!" over and over again, sobbing, "Flox, you dear, good Floxie!" The two of them, boy and dog, wept for joy and huddled tightly together, while Jan scratched the dog behind the ears and Flox put his paws on the boy's shoulders.

"Flox, what have you been doing? Were you looking for Vladimir? He's gone to the war, and they've left us on our own. Have you seen Grocer Kaczmar's poor old sow? Come on, Flox, you're mine now and I'm yours. You're the best person in the world! Listen to them firing, those Germans! They've blown up that great plum tree — what did it ever do to them? And they've shot off the pig's leg — isn't that mean! Come on, Flox, don't be afraid. I'm here with you, come on!" The shaggy-haired dog had already run through the open door into the back room, with Jan behind him, and from there to the kitchen. There Flox got up on his hind legs and sniffed eagerly at the larder, wagging his tail and barking. Jan understood that language: "Bow-wow! Bow-wow!" went the dog. It sounded like: Now, now! Now, now! There was something on a shelf high up, a big brown bowl and a wooden spoon beside it. Jan stood on his toes, reaching carefully for the covered bowl and lowering it carefully, too, because there was something lapping inside. Flox sat quite tense and still.

Jan removed the cloth and both of them gave their own exclamations of delight: "Sour cream, sour cream!" "Bow-wow!"

They fell to, drinking from the same bowl, Jan with the spoon and Flox with his tongue, sharing fairly, like brothers. Flox licked out the bottom on his own.

Strengthened and comforted, they rummaged around the kitchen and went on foraging through the pantry and living room. First they found a few matches and a candle end, then an old calendar, a blue kitchen apron, and finally even a mouth organ, which still made the right notes: *Hoooo-toooo, hoooo-toooo.* Flox sniffed at the candle end, Jan looked at the greasy calendar and there — suddenly he realized: today was his birthday. Really! Today was September 14, and it was already coming to an end.

Jan was glad he had at least managed to save the very tip of his birthday. "Flox," he called, "I'm fourteen today!" and he blew a fanfare on the mouth organ. The firing stopped.

"Flox, it's my birthday! Come on, wish me a happy birthday; give me your paw!" Flox sat back on his haunches, and because he was happy that his friend was happy, he gave him both paws at once. The dog looked into the boy's eyes with the loyalty that only a dog's eyes can express and with an alertness that seemed to say: "Jan, watch out for people. They're not to be relied on. They shoot without knowing who gets hit. They kill without knowing why. I wish you luck, my Jan; I think you need it, my friend!"

But Jan understood little of that silent dog language. Gently he thrust his hands into Flox's woolly coat. "Your coat should be clipped, Flox. I think you need it, my friend!"

But first there was the birthday table to be set. In the past his mother had done it, his dear mother, the best mother in the village. No other boy in Kopchovka had ever had a birthday party. She had prepared the last one for him. But before the first snow had fallen she was dead and now she lay out in the cemetery behind the village. Now Jan wanted to do things in the same way as his mother had that last time. He brushed away the fat, black flies and laid the blue apron on the table as a cloth. Then came the presents: the old calendar that had given him the idea, the mouth organ as the *pièce de résistance,* and for a birthday cake the brown milk bowl. There was no milk left in it, but it was a very happy memory for both Jan and Flox.

Jan planted the candle end in the middle of the bowl and struck one of the matches.

How beautifully the light shone, reflected warmly in the dog's eyes, as they followed Jan's movements earnestly. It was really festive. The sun sank behind the birches by the Ravka Bridge. Now it was time for an expedition into the village, Jan thought, for he was not yet full. The dog, which had had the same idea for some time, jumped up at him excitedly. Jan took the mouth organ off the table and blew into it: *Toooo-hooo, toooo* — but he broke off in midnote, as if the instrument had suddenly snapped in two. He stood motionless, listening, his cheerful mood gone as surely as the plum tree. Flox had dropped his tail and was whining softly.

From the distance they heard a muffled shouting, coming closer and closer. It must be them, the Germans, from whom the entire village and all the Russian soldiers with their rifles and cannon had been running! "Rah! Rah!" yelled the terrible soldiers, louder and louder: "Rah — rah — hurrah!"

As the noise grew, so did Jan's fear. He climbed, shaking, onto the big stove and crept onto the backmost corner. Now it's all over, he thought. Like an insect playing dead when a pursuer approaches, Jan pressed himself flat on top of the stove. He had pulled Flox up beside him. He was now his only defense.

He pulled a couple of ragged sacks he had found up there over himself and his companion. Perhaps they would not be noticed.

Heavy footsteps came toward the inn. Now they were echoing in the passage. The door to the taproom opened.

"Anyone here?" called a hoarse voice. Jan did not move. The dog also played dead. A miserable heap of rags with one human and one animal soul waited for the end.

❖ JAN BECOMES
A GUN BEAST

THERE ARE ALL KINDS OF GUNS, BUT ALL HAVE the same purpose: to kill men and destroy human property. There are light and heavy guns, small ones and enormous ones; there are guns that shoot at close range and guns with such a long range that the naked eye cannot see whom the shot has hit and what it has destroyed. There are guns that shoot upward at aircraft, which burst into flames and plunge thousands of feet down to earth. There are guns that shoot over the sea. They sink ships and all their crew and the goods they're carrying: grain, wood, cotton, machines, and even money.

Cannon shells fly in an arc like a thrown stone, or a ball; this arc is called a trajectory. Many trajectories are only slightly curved, like a bridge or an eyebrow, others more like a rainbow.

But however many types of guns and trajectories there are, guns never go off by themselves. People have to be there first, to aim them in the direction where the shots are to fall. Those people have to load every shell

13

in the gun correctly and, finally, there has to be the one who fires the gun.

The people who do this are known as the artillery.

The artillery serve the guns, which are their masters. The guns that had yesterday demolished the plum tree and Panie Ostrovsky's barn, Uncle Peter's house, and many other things were served by twenty gunners, and these twenty gunners now lay squeezed close together on the narrow taproom floor, snoring. They had pulled off their heavy boots and set them at their feet; their leather belts, from which hung a brownish haversack together with two black bags and a short saber or side arm, lay beside them. For pillows they had their packs, which looked rather like schoolbags, stuffed with laundry, cleaning things, soap, a pair of shoes, biscuits, and preserves. They also contained a prayer book, setting out the Creed and the commandments and a number of beautiful prayers, such as: "Lord, give peace in our time. Lead our feet into the way of peace! Lamb of God, Thou that takest away the sins of the world, grant us Thy peace!" Besides these, each gunner had a rifle.

These rifles, also known as carbines, leaned against the wall, and since no one was using them, they did no one any harm. They slept.

Twenty carbines slept, and twenty gunners snored and dreamed, and sometimes one turned over in his dream, shoving his neighbor as he did so. His neighbor shoved back, growled something, and went on dreaming.

One dreamed of his little daughter climbing on his

knee, grabbing at his great black beard and playing with it. But what was really tickling him was no little daughter. It was not the hands of his little Freda. It was the foul lice that take an enthusiastic part in every war and attack every soldier, whether he is fighting for or against Germany.

The bearded man's neighbor, a young, pale-faced gunner with a delicate skin, called Behr, was dreaming himself back at school, in the swimming pool, dangling his legs in the water and talking to his classmates, who splashed around him, about his march through the mud in Russian Poland. Bathing, bathing! That was his only dream.

Corn, corn, his neighbor dreamed, and walked across his fields through the corn and was happy. Each of them had a different dream, but every dream was of home. They smiled in their sleep. The war had not been going on for very long — only since the second of August. Now it was the fifteenth of September. Scarcely one of the gunners could imagine that he would not be home by Christmas. That was what the supreme commander had promised, and these good people believed him: home again for Christmas.

The fifteenth of September, 1914, dawned. The sun had risen, but the gunners still slept and would no doubt have gone on sleeping for some time, when there was a sudden thud. "Ouch, damn me!" shouted the fat gunner Albin Rosenlöcher. "Ouch, it's raining cobbler's boys!"

When he opened his eyes, he saw that it really was a

ragged boy who had fallen straight down on him from above, for Gunner Rosenlöcher was lying right up against the stove.

"Watch what you're doing, you miserable bedbug!" he shouted. "If I wasn't so tired I'd box your ears. Can't you find something else to sit on besides my head?" He would have gone on, but the other soldiers had been wakened by the noisy arrival, and when they saw what had happened they all began to shout at once: "Look at that!" cried one, "Fat Rosie's had a baby in the night!" . . . "Congratulations, congratulations, Papa Rosenlöcher! A strapping boy, just like his dad!" The taproom echoed with laughter, until Rosenlöcher had to join in. Jan had no idea what was happening. He must have turned over in his sleep and fallen off the stove, and now he stood in the midst of the hubbub, not daring to move a muscle.

When twenty soldiers laugh at a poor, sleepy boy, it's no laughing matter for him, especially when he is in the state Jan was in. His shirt was so filthy that there was no telling whether it had once been grey, red, or brown. The left shoulder and right sleeve were torn, and the trousers hanging round his legs were more holes than cloth. And his feet! There was so much mud on them that there was no skin to be seen. It was lucky he could not see his own face, or he would have been still more ashamed. Under the flaxen hair, bright blue eyes looked out from broad crisscross lines of black, like a bad piece of homework crossed out by the teacher.

When the laughter had died down a little, Rosenlöcher said, "Well, boy, what do you want? Anything to report? Don't be frightened, nobody here's going to hurt you or he'll feel the back of my hand. What are you doing here?" He spoke in the dialect of his native Saxony, and Jan gaped in bewilderment. In Kopchovka they spoke quite a different German, and he couldn't understand what the Saxon was saying.

"Who are you?" he asked hesitantly.

"What are we? Gunners, what else? Royal Prussian Artillery," they all shouted at once.

Jan still could not understand properly. "But you're men, aren't you?" he said.

"Men. Do you think we're monkeys?" said the bearded man.

"They said you were gun beasts," said Jan with an awkward smile.

Then they really laughed: "Hahahaha! Did you hear that? Gun beasts! Hohoho! This boy is good, heeheehee! Gun beasts, hahahaaaa hoho!"

"Bow-wow-wow-wow! Bow-wow-wow!" Their laughter was drowned by frenzied barking. Flox was barking from the stove in a great rage, standing with legs braced and teeth bared, as if preparing to spring at every laughing throat.

"What sort of a little polar bear is that?" said Rosenlöcher, laughing, and the bearded man added, "That's no polar bear, it's a raccoon. Look at the stripes!"

"But he's like you, Distelmann!" put in tall Hottenrot, and he sniggered.

"Oh, how's that?" growled the bearded man.

"Well, we can't see your nose for hair either, man!"

"Get him out of here!" shouted a skinny man called Senf. "He's a walking flea barracks!" And he pulled on his boots hastily.

Little Behr, who had been dreaming of the swimming pool and was now polishing his horn-rimmed glasses, surveyed Flox through them for a moment. "It's a cross between a mudpie and a bedside rug."

The entertainment was interrupted by the sudden opening of the door to the back room. A firm, suntanned face, with bright, intelligent eyes gazed at the confused scene. It belonged to a young man whose long legs were covered with shining brown leather. Over his grey-green soldier's tunic hung a black-and-white iron cross on a black-and-white ribbon. This was the first lieutenant. His men had nicknamed him the White Raven, because he had his own opinion about everything, and that is as rare among the military as a raven with white feathers. His real name was Hans Alert.

"What's all this row about?" he asked.

"Beg to report, sir," said one of the men, grinning and standing stiff as a broom, "Rosenlöcher's had a baby."

"What's that?"

"And Distelmann's had a little dog, sir," said Rosenlöcher. "The resemblance is posi*tive*ly startling!"

"Stop sniggering!" ordered the officer, trying to keep his face straight. Then, turning to Jan, "What's your name?"

"Jan, panie!"

"Jan Panie?" repeated the lieutenant. "What a funny name."

"No, panie," Jan corrected him, "my name is *Jan*, panie."

"I don't get it. Your name is not Jan Panie and your name *is* Jan Panie. Now, out with it! First name?"

"Jan, panie."

"Right then: Jan. We'll leave the Panie. And your surname?"

"Kubitzky, panie."

"If you say *panie* to me once more . . . ! Call me uncle if you like!"

"No, panie, not uncle!" said Jan hastily, pulling a face.

"Why not, blockhead?"

Jan hesitated. "My uncle always hits me."

"Then call me lieutenant, understand?"

"Yes, Panie Lieutenant." The gunners were sniggering again.

"It's either *sir* or *lieutenant*, not *panie lieutenant!*"

"Yes, pan — Sir Lieutenant."

"Oh, that's enough. What sort of a brute's that up there?"

"That's not a brute, Sir Lieutenant, that's my friend Flox." Flox jumped down from the stove.

"Are you from this village, you and your friend?" asked Alert.

"Yes, Sir Lieutenant."

"You're alone here?" Jan nodded. "Alone under our fire?"

Jan nodded again. "The Russian soldiers were shooting at the village, too."

"That must have been damned uncomfortable, don't

you think?" said the White Raven, looking around at his men, who were now staring thoughtfully at the boy. And after a pause: "Humph, you're our prisoner then. Hm! Our one and only prisoner after our heroic capture of Kopchovka!"

Jan started at the word "prisoner." Prisoner? he thought — but only thieves and criminals or rabid dogs are put in prison! He hadn't committed a crime, had he? The panie had been so friendly just now, but now — prisoner?

"Do you speak Polish, boy?" asked the officer.

"Yes, Sir Lieutenant, I have to."

"Have to? Why?"

"Because the squire speaks Polish and my uncle and Mrs. Goloborotka and — "

"Naturally," said Alert, turning to the door. "Well, we'll see what we can make of it. Above all, give the boy something to eat! You're hungry, I suppose?"

"Yes, Sir Lieutenant, and Flox is, too."

As soon as the White Raven had gone, the noise and confusion broke out again, one man missing a sock, one a tie or a button. Little Behr had lost his watch and claimed that Flox had swallowed it. Everyone was cursing, but suddenly everything was in its right place, including the watch, only the cursing went on. Now they were cursing the war, the damned war.

"Why do you have a war then?" asked Jan. "If it's damned?"

"Stupid kid!" said Distelmann. "Because we have to. Think anyone asked us?"

Jan understood that. His own father had had to, as well. But Rosenlöcher, brushing his hair, shouted: "We're fighting for king and fatherland. We're never going to stop!" And he passed his comb to Jan, who tried to get his blond mop under control. "We're fighting for German civilization, little Panie," said Fritz Behr. That Jan did not understand.

"You're all fighting for one thing: *the skull of the African Sultan Mkwawa.*" Everyone gazed in wonder at the speaker, a tall, muscular man with tanned skin and brown hair, going grey at the temples.

"For what, Cordes? Whose skull? *What* was the sultan called?" they shouted.

"Oh, it's just one of those stories from Africa. It just occurred to me. I spent eight years down in the colonies, remember."

"Fire away then, Cordes!" said Rosenlöcher. "I'm interested in African things. Were they cannibals?"

"I'll tell you another time," said the other. "Now I'm going to have a wash."

He thrust a black metal pot into Jan's hands. "Get some water, little Panie, come on! You can wash yourself at the same time. There: soap. But bring it back, do you hear?"

"You can bring a liter back for Papa, too," said Rosenlöcher, putting a second pot in Jan's other hand. "Then you won't be down on one side."

Jan would have preferred to eat first—the lieutenant had talked about food—but he thought it wisest to obey. When he opened the door, Flox shot out between his legs.

Jan had intended to go to the well behind Uncle Peter's house, but there were so many soldiers around it. Perhaps his uncle was looking for him and would beat him. He went down to the Ravka instead. There was no need to dip for the water there; he could simply plunge in feet first.

Oh, but it felt wonderful! The water of the Ravka turned dark with all the mud.

Then Flox arrived and was scrubbed, rubbed down, soaped, and rinsed. He kept still with great patience, as if he were carved out of wood. Only when Jan soaped his muzzle did he lick off all the foam. The water of the Ravka turned black a second time.

Now Jan was sitting in the inn like a grown man with the soldiers around him. He had a thick slice of bread in one hand. "Here's something to spread on it," said Papa Rosenlöcher with a grin, pushing a tin across to him. "But not too thick, my son. That's butter from a real cow, that is."

In the middle of the room Flox sat back on his hindquarters and snuffled. Each of the men gave him a morsel of bread, and Jan actually gave him two, making twenty-two gulps in all. They tasted better than soapsuds.

"Now, men," said the lieutenant, coming in from the street, "how do you like it? You've got a new comrade now." Then, to Jan, "What about it, boy, want to stay with us? You must know your way about and you speak Polish, too. You could be useful to us."

Jan turned red with pride and pleasure. He must be

quite a fellow, to be made an offer like that! But what would his uncle say? Nothing. He would beat him until he could neither sit nor lie down for three days.

"I'd like to, sir," he said haltingly, "I would like . . . but . . . my uncle . . ."

"He'd beat you if you told him?" Embarrassed, Jan did not answer. "I could have a word with him," said the White Raven, "or do you think he'd beat me, too? Where is he?"

Jan shrugged. "I don't know, sir. They all ran away from you."

Hottenrot, the tall man, laughed. "We thought the whole village was full of Russkis, and there wasn't so much as a pig left."

"There was," Jan contradicted him. "Grocer Kaczmar's pig, the one whose leg you shot off. Couldn't we help the poor creature?"

"He's already been helped," said Hottenrot happily, glancing at little Behr.

Behr said, "It's going the way of all pork: into the cook pot."

"You'll get a slice too, my son," said Rosenlöcher.

"Think it over then," said the officer, patting Jan's blond head. "There's plenty of time. We'll be staying here for the time being." Then, to his men, "Make sure you're prepared. The battery is to be mounted behind the village. Report ready for firing by eight."

Funny words they use, thought Jan. Battery? Mounted? I don't understand. What does it all mean?

But it must have meant a lot, because Alert had scarcely spoken before the whole taproom came to life.

Each man stuffed the last bit of bread into his mouth, buckled on his leather equipment, and ran outside, headed by Flox.

What's the matter with the dog, thought Jan. He's gone completely mad. First he rushed across to Uncle Peter's house, where there was still a crowd of soldiers, then came slowly back, tail down, pressed against Jan's legs, and nudged him with his muzzle. Afterward he ran off again toward the ruined house. Jan followed him, slipping through the crowd.

Holy Mother of God, what was that? A shudder ran through his body and he turned hot and cold. There in the rubble, among charred slats and planks, lay Uncle Peter, full length on his back and barefooted. There were clumps of black flies on his burned hands and the brandy bottle that Jan had fetched from the inn for him the day before lay broken beside him.

"He was drunk when he got his," said a voice, and another, "For goodness sake, put him in a length of canvas!" — "There's a lime pit behind, push him in there!" came from the other side.

Jan stood as if paralyzed. Although the village street was full of sunshine, he was frozen to the marrow. The soldiers laid the dead man on the grey-green canvas and picked him up. The hands that had hit Jan so often stuck out threateningly under the cloth, which sagged toward the earth like a heavy sack.

"What are you doing here, youngster?" asked a broad-shouldered man with gold braid and a big stud in his collar. Jan could not say a word. But suddenly he heard the kind voice of his Papa Rosenlöcher: "This is

our Jan, Sergeant, and what a brave lad he is! He was
the only person in the whole place in all that shooting
yesterday."

"Except for this one," said the sergeant, indicating
Uncle Peter's corpse as it disappeared around the corner of the house. "Did you know him?"

Jan nodded. "My uncle."

"You don't say! Your uncle!" Rosenlöcher consoled
him. "Keep your chin up, lad. He can't beat you up
anymore, you can do what you like now, you don't
have to ask him if you can come with us. None of us is
going to beat you, I'll see to that. I'm your papa now."
So saying, he took Jan's hand, and as they walked down
the street toward the field he told him about his own
boy at home in Saxony, his Oscar. "Like to see a picture of him? There!" And he pulled a photograph out
of his grey tunic. It showed a boy with precisely the
same good-humored, full-moon face as Papa Rosenlöcher, his right foot on the pedal of a bicycle, as if he
were about to jump on. "If you ever happen to be in
Plauen, you must drop in. We've got a grocery store,"
he added proudly.

"Can I ride the bike, too?" asked Jan, forgetting
about his uncle.

"Of course," said Papa.

"Papa!" Jan shrieked in horror, pointing across the
field. "Those are cannon!" Before them stood four grey
monsters, the barrels with their sinister mouths aimed
straight at the approaching pair.

"They won't hurt you. Not if the lieutenant and me
don't want them to — "

"Jan!" called the lieutenant, catching sight of them. He was sitting on a grey-painted box beside the cannon. Jan ran over to him. On his knees the officer had a map on which he was tracing a line with his finger. "Tell me, Jan, you must know where Pollnow is, don't you?"

"Over there!" said Jan, pointing out the direction.

"Good! Now, do you happen to know of a place near here from which Pollnow would be visible?" Jan remembered a pine tree that he had once climbed to get a crow's nest. He had seen Pollnow at the same time.

"There's a tree," he said, "not far from here. If you climb up it — "

"It shall be done," the lieutenant interrupted him. "You can take us there right away."

"Can Flox come, too?" asked Jan.

In a few minutes a small procession was moving across the fields. Flox ran in front, then came the White Raven with Jan, and a soldier dragging a stand and a big case containing, as Jan discovered when he asked, a telescope. Two more soldiers were carrying a long ladder.

"Are you a gunner, too?" Jan asked the man with the telescope.

"No, little Panie, I'm a lance corporal, a noncommissioned officer."

"Do you shoot the cannon as well?"

"No," said the lance corporal, "I make observations through this telescope. I see if the others have aimed right and hit the target."

"Then you must have seen that I was alone in the village. Why didn't you tell the others they weren't aiming right?"

The proud lance corporal fell silent, but Alert, who had been listening to the short exchange, said, "The boy's all right. Well, how about it, Jan? Will you stay with us?"

"If you'll let me, sir. There's the tree." He pointed to a pine tree rising out of the bushes ahead of them.

The soldiers placed the ladder against the tree, took the telescope from its case, and hoisted it carefully into the branches. Soon Jan was sitting up there with Alert and the telescope, pointing out the church spire of Pollnow and everything else the lieutenant wanted to know. The lieutenant listened attentively, and Flox, sitting at the foot of the pine, also gazed expectantly upward.

When Jan, nimble as a squirrel, climbed down again, Alert gave him a look that was both kind and admiring and repeated, "The boy's all right." Then, to the lance corporal: "Häberlein, fit the young man out: tunic, socks, shoes, and above all clean linen! You're a good boy, Jan, and you shouldn't be running around in rags, not if you're going to stay with us. You can have your hair cut at the same time."

"Can Flox, too, sir?"

Behind the cannon there was a truck in the field, stuffed with all kinds of things and covered with canvas tarpaulins. This was the gunners' traveling wardrobe.

"Ever seen a gunner as small as this? Ain't no such thing!" chortled the quartermaster sergeant when Lance Corporal Häberlein asked for clothes and underclothes for Jan. After lengthy searching and trying on, they did find a pair of trousers that only had to be folded up a matter of five inches at the bottom. The underclothes, tunic, and shoes were also something to be grown into and as far as the cap was concerned, it was a good thing Jan had two ears on his head; otherwise his headgear would have fallen onto the tip of his nose. But according to the quartermaster everything fitted perfectly. "Like a first-class Berlin tailor!" said Häberlein, laughing, and gave the order: "Left about turn, forward to the barber!"

A barber soldier was standing at the ready, clashing his big scissors. "Flox first!" Jan begged.

"And Panie next. Don't you think you're going to escape us!" threatened Häberlein. Then he seized the dog, who was growling distrustfully at the barber's scissors.

Talk about hard work!

When about two pounds of wool were lying on the ground, Häberlein suddenly shouted with surprise, "Man, it's a poodle! I thought it was a sheep that could bark."

"I saw right off that it was a poodle," said the barber importantly. "In fact, it's a king poodle. My aunt had one. I would never have thought king poodles were bred in these parts. Now I'm going to cut him two pairs of perfect cuffs and a mane! I tell you, if he ever goes to Africa, everyone will think he's a lion."

Jan was transformed, too. When Papa held a piece of mirror glass in front of his face, he wondered at first who it was. A soldier looked back at him — one of the German soldiers from whom the whole of Kopchovka had fled, of whom he had been scared to death — and that soldier was himself, Jan. He still could not believe it.

Rosenlöcher had been watching his protégé from the side. Now he put his hand on Jan's shoulder and said, "You see, my son, you've turned into a gun beast, too!"

❖ WHAT ARE THE SOLDIERS GOING TO EAT?

ONCE A GUN HAS FIRED, A FEW SECONDS MUST elapse before it can fire again. The gunners have to replace the shell with a new one and the gunlayer has to reaim the barrel toward the spot where the shot should land. For a few seconds the cannons are silent and at peace, but human beings do not want peace, even for five seconds, so they mount several cannon side by side and aim them all at the target. While the first weapon is at peace, the second is firing, then the rest, and when the last has shot the first is ready to fire again.

A combination of four or six cannon with everything they need in the way of people and horses, gun carriages, and shells, is called a battery. A combination of several heavy batteries makes up a battalion of artillery. The battery Jan had met in such a curious way moved off on Saturday, the nineteenth of September, 1914, through Pollnow, the village whose church spire Jan had pointed out on the day after the destruction of Kopchovka. They were moving steadily eastward, following the Russians.

30

Two hundred and fifty gunners marched, knapsacks and rifles on their backs, helmets on their heads, through the deep sand behind their officers, guns, and munition wagons. A thick cloud of dust lay above the wagon train, moving as they marched. The lieutenant was riding ahead on a brown mare as they left Kopchovka at five in the morning. Now it was five in the afternoon, the hooves of the draught horses were dragging through the sandy soil, the gunners' stomachs were rumbling, and through their ranks ran one word, the commonest word in the soldier's language: starving!

At the next halt Alert said, "In about two hours we should be there. If little Panie has given Jakob the right directions, the supply wagon should be there before us. There will be mail and cigars, too, that's the main thing. We can hold out till then. Sing!" he ordered.

And little Behr broke out in his clear voice:

What are the soldiers going to eat,
Captain and Lieutenant, say?
Carrots and peas with good roast meat,
That's what the soldiers are going to eat:
Captain, Lieutenant,
Corporal, Sergeant,
Take the maiden,
Take the maiden by the hand,
Soldiers,
Comrades,
Take the maiden,
Take the maiden by the hand!

Now there wasn't a maiden to be seen far and wide, nor any meat, either roast or boiled, either with or without carrots and peas, but a song is always a good thing. A song keeps your heart up. The whole battery joined in. Their pace became firmer, the dust eddied higher, hunger and tiredness seemed forgotten.

What are the soldiers going to drink
Captain and Lieutenant, say?
The very best wine that you can think,
That's what the soldiers are going to drink. . . .

Jan had left with Corporal Jakob and the supply wagon at 4:45 A.M., heading for Gradicz. Flox, too, of course. He was lying in the wagon on a pile of empty sacks, fast asleep, but Jan was sitting on the box beside the driver, a soldier called Schnabel, showing him the way. *Schnabel* means beak, and this Schnabel had a high, twittering voice, so the others called him Bird-beak. The corporal sat on the bench inside the wagon, studying a map, but it meant little to him.

They moved at a slow trot through deserted fields beside the Ravka. There was not a peasant, not a cow to be seen; only frogs and toads croaked in the tussocks and pools.

At a walking pace they passed through Trabcine, which consisted of two lines of squalid huts. Here they were met by other military wagons from different divisions, also heading for Gradicz to receive meat, bread, salt, cooking fat, sugar, coffee, and tobacco for the soldiers, and feed for the horses. If only they had known the way! No one could make anything of the maps, but

as soon as they heard that Jan knew his way about the
area, they called, "Come on then, young Hindenburg*!" Schnabel cracked his whip, the procession set
off, Jan showing them the way through the broad,
trackless forests of Vielki.

Toward noon the road reappeared. The forest was at
an end. They were approaching the small town of Gradicz. More and more soldiers appeared, more and more
wagons. Sometimes the traffic reached a complete
standstill. They had to hug the right-hand edge of the
road, for on the left an equal crowd was moving in the
opposite direction: long grey lines of soldiers, cannon,
cannon, soldiers, all shrouded in dust.

"That's the Eighteenth Division," said Jakob. The
world seemed full of German soldiers.

Cars passed, too. Jan was confused, for he had never
seen a car before. In one sat a glittering soldier, his uniform all gold and red; only his hair was grey. Jakob explained that this was the general who gave orders to all
the soldiers and officers Jan had seen. For although all
this was part of the Eighteenth Division, it was far from
the whole of it and the Eighteenth Division was, after
all, only the eighteenth. There were another seventeen
before it, just as big, and some more after it, though he
did not know how many. Jan felt dizzy. It was true, the
whole world *was* full of German soldiers.

More cars, with more glittering officers.

"I'd like to have a chance of living like them!" piped
Birdbeak. "They should try trudging along on foot all

* Paul von Hindenburg (1847–1934): Commander-in-chief of the
German Army in World War I.

day, with blisters and a heavy shooter and a monkey on their backs!"

"Monkey?" asked Jan eagerly. "Where are the monkeys?" He peered about him while Jakob and Birdbeak collapsed with laughter.

"Take a good look!" said the corporal. "There, monkeys! A forest of monkeys!" Then Jan saw that he meant the brown packs that seemed to cling to the soldiers' backs. Still laughing, they drove into Gradicz.

The place had never seen a day like this one. Through the small station rolled endless goods trains, which were unloaded and shunted to and fro. Heavy trucks stopped beside the trains to take on vast quantities of supplies and rattled off fully laden to the marketplace to distribute their loads to the waiting troop wagons.

This was easier said than done, for in the marketplace there was such a coming and going of men and vehicles that nothing could move in or out. There were such shouts and curses, whistles and bellows, mooing and neighing that you could not hear yourself speak. Not even Flox's loud barking penetrated the din. Only one small, shaggy cur pricked up its ears and went tail-wagging to meet the poodle. Flox accepted the invitation and leaped boldly down from the wagon, glad of canine company at last. "Watch out he doesn't get pinched, Panie," said Birdbeak. Jan watched out.

Meanwhile, Jakob had taken over the reins himself and maneuvered the wagon through the tumult, making straight for the mountain of human and animal food that had been stacked at the furthest corner of the square. The other drivers and corporals — who must already have been waiting a long time — followed him with their curses, but Jakob took no notice. He drove on.

At last they reached the food mountain. Behind them surged a heaving sea of waiting wagons. But without looking back, Jakob made straight for the full packing cases and sacks and the soldiers distributing them. One of them sat behind a table keeping a record. Jakob handed over a requisition with Alert's signature on it.

But suddenly an elegant young man in a brand-new, light-grey tunic with a high collar barred his way. In his right eye was a round monocle, in his right hand a riding whip. "Where from? What battery?" he snarled at Jakob.

"Seventh Battery, Seventeenth Battalion," said Jakob, irritably. What was this dandy playing at? The information was on the requisition he had handed over to the recording soldier.

"You can wait," said the young man with the monocle, flourishing his whip in the air.

"No, sir, I can't, unfortunately," said Jakob. "I must get to my battery. That's more than four hours away, and if I have to wait here — "

"Then you have to wait," the lieutenant interrupted him. "I'm not wasting my time, either."

"I should hope not," retorted Jakob with a faint smile.

Oh, but the hero with the riding crop went for Jakob, his face purple, and yelled so terribly that for a moment

Jan saw his Uncle Peter before his very eyes. But even his uncle could not roar like this: "Are you crazy, you dirty Jew, you!"

"Aha!" went Jakob.

"Shut up!" snorted the fine gentleman. "Getting bumptious, are we? I shan't forget you. You've picked the wrong man this time." And to the soldiers in charge of the distribution, he commanded, "The Jew gets it last, after all the rest, understand?" Then, to Jakob, "There, now you can get another bawling out from your battery commander because you're late! Enjoy your meal!" He struck the horse pulling Jakob's wagon on the nose with his crop and walked off.

But he did not get far. In five strides Jakob had overtaken him, barred his way, and said, "That I simply won't have, sir!"

"What . . ." said the man, struggling for words. "You . . . dare to contradict me? I'll have you arrested on the spot, on — the — spot! I've never seen such impertinence. Do you know what it means to contradict a superior officer? Insubordination, mutiny before an assembled company. In wartime, the penalty is death. You'll find out who you're dealing with!"

Jan was terrified, but Jakob looked the furious man calmly in the face, took two short paces toward him, and bowed. "I don't have to find out, I know exactly who you are, Herr Heribert König. I am Doctor Jakob, legal counsel."

The other man shrank — as if he were a defendant, thought Birdbeak.

Jakob spoke, softly, every word distinct: "Perhaps my name is familiar to you from the past. But never mind the past. This horse is the property of the German Army. You struck it. You have not yet struck the enemy. You've shirked that. You'd rather strike a poor animal that has been pulling a wagon since five o'clock in the morning. Where were *you* at five o'clock this morning? I will tell you: in the so-called Harmless Club with Captain Tziecke. It's *you* who have picked the wrong man. Unless I get twenty pounds extra oats for this unfortunate animal, right now, the High Command will receive a report on your behavior this very day, and your comfortable armchair job will be a thing of the past."

The young man turned pale. "Sir — " he stuttered, "I . . . I don't think I can be hearing properly. You are speaking to a superior — "

"Quickly, please," said Jakob. "My time is precious, the men are waiting. Will you or won't you? I can be with the High Command in ten minutes." He signaled to Schnabel to turn the wagon, and Birdbeak took up the reins to obey.

Then the last thing Jan had expected happened.

As if it were nothing out of the ordinary, the lieutenant called one of the men and ordered him to deal with Jakob straight away and to add an extra twenty pounds of oats. Then he raised his crop in greeting and vanished like a snuffed-out candle.

Next the fully laden wagon drove along a narrow alley into a courtyard with a manger standing in it.

Schnabel poured in oats, and Jakob added a generous amount of the extra rations he had just obtained.

Flox had parted from his new acquaintance with a heavy heart. Now he received an end of sausage to cheer him up. Some pale-faced, hollow-eyed children stood around the courtyard and stared.

Jakob went through the back entrance into a small shop where he had some purchases to make for his comrades in the battery: thread and writing paper, knives and trouser-buttons, chocolate, bootlaces, handkerchiefs, suspenders, and above all, tobacco. No soldier can ever get enough tobacco.

At a table to the rear of the shop sat a white-haired old man with a long beard and a yellowish face from which projected a narrow, high-bridged nose. He wore a small black cap under which his hair hung down in long curls. He was wearing the dark, old-fashioned dress of a Polish Jew.

"Oy-yoy-yoy-yoy-yoy," he said, shaking his head, as Jakob, Jan, and Birdbeak entered the low room. "Oy-yoy-yoy! German soldiers come, buying today, Sabbath. Gentlemen excuse, I take no money, Sabbath. Jew not work Sabbath, not sell, no business."

"Very well," said Jakob, who knew all about it. "We don't want to do business with you. We just want to take what we need. We'll leave the money here, on the table, and you can take it when you like. But there's no harm in your telling us what things cost. There's nothing in the Law against that."

"German officers very clever," said the old man, "clever men, fine men! German officers won't rob me."

As if they were ordinary shoppers, the three went around finding all the things they needed while the old man sat where he was, never taking his eyes off the visitors. At last he stood up and turned to Jakob with a polite smile. "The officer will excuse a question. . . ."

"Well?"

"No offense, officer. I'm an old Jew, I don't see well, only asking the officer — " There was an awkward pause.

"Well, what is it?"

"I had a nephew, God keep him. He is dead. He had eyes and mouth and nose, all the face — just like the officer's."

"For heaven's sake," said Jakob, laughing, "you're not trying to say we're related?"

"God forbid, how can old Abraham from Gradicz be relation with fine German officer? Only I thought: from forefathers, perhaps, from Abraham, Isaac, and Jacob, the officer must excuse me, I mean: is the officer perhaps a Jew?"

"Well, in the first place," said Jakob, "I'm not an officer, only a corporal — "

"Corporal excuse, old Abraham he knows from Law and faces better than uniforms."

"Your eyes didn't deceive you, Abraham," said Jakob. "My forefathers and yours once wore the same uniform in the blessed land."

The old man was transformed in a flash. Taking a step toward his fellow Jew, he spoke earnestly and sternly, like a father. "And now you wear *that* uniform, my son? Have you not learned the commandment:

Thou shalt not kill? Why have you become a soldier, my son?"

"I must, Abraham," said Jakob. "In Germany every man must become a soldier."

"You must? What means: you must?" asked the old man, almost chanting. "Was not in Germany once a great man, a great poet, who wrote in the book and that book I have read myself with mine own eyes: 'No man must.' No man must — a good word, a true word."

Then Jan, who had been listening attentively, although he sometimes had difficulty in understanding the old Jew's strange accent, asked, "What about children? Mustn't they obey?"

"A clever boy!" said the old man. "Boy, hear this: no man must, unless he *will*. Children must obey their mother and their father because they *want to*, because they are one heart and one soul and one will. Have you once seen a single mother who has said to her child: go forth and be shot dead? Has your mother commanded you to put on that tunic and go around with the soldiers? Or have you perhaps no mother now?"

Jan nodded. "I have no other tunic, either."

"Poor boy!" said the old man.

There was silence in the little room. Jakob laid the suspenders he had just found on the table and said, "No, Father Abraham, no man must. But I don't want people to say the Jews are cowards."

"What is coward? You need more courage than a whole regiment of soldiers to say: I shall not touch a gun, I shall not shoot. You need more courage for that than to run about with the others and shoot with the others at the children of the fathers and mothers who brought them up in care and sorrow. Listen, my son: if with your gun and with your cannon you shoot dead a thousand people and more — what good is that to you? None, it is I who tell you, old Abraham. You Germans will fight and conquer, conquer and fight, for years and years, and at the last you will have lost. And if it were otherwise, if you had won the war with God's help and yours, what do you think the mighty ones in Germany would say? Heh? They would say: now we make a new war, a war that costs nothing and brings money. Now we make a war against the Jews. Against the Jews in our country. And then they will make a war against you and all your people and destroy your house and kill your wife. And that will be their thanks to you for wearing that bloody uniform."

"Are you a prophet?" asked Jakob.

"Prophet? Why do I need to be a prophet when I have a head that thinks and two eyes that see?"

Birdbeak, who had paid little attention to this conversation, had finished his search: "I'm going to dash over to the field post office," he said. "Coming, Jan?"

But Jan preferred to stay with Jakob and Abraham and their talk.

Jakob placed the money for the goods on the table. "Farewell, Father Abraham!"

"Go with God!" murmured the old man. "Don't get yourself shot and don't shoot anyone else, so that you come home to your father's house happy, with a clear conscience. Where do you come from, my son?"

"From Frankfurt," said Jakob.

"Frankfurt?" repeated the old man, his face lighting up as though he spoke of a distant fairyland. "Frankfurt, that is well for you, my son!" And lowering his voice secretively: "There is one of our community who was once in Frankfurt: the Reb Kolischer. He was a good man, a wise teacher, but he has been ill, very ill, and we thought he must die. Then the whole community put their money together and sent him to a famous doctor who lives in Frankfurt and the Reb made the long journey until he came to the River Main, where the famous doctor lives. And that one made him well, so that he could continue to read the Law and teach our children. But when he asked the doctor, 'What does it cost you to have healed me? The community will pay,' the doctor said, 'Take your money back. I know your community is poor. Give the money to the poor!' Do you hear, my son, that is what the great doctor from Germany said to the Reb from Poland in Russia. And because you are from Frankfurt, you shall be blessed. But remember the commandment!"

"It's time, Corporal!" called Birdbeak through the doorway. He was carrying a heavy sack on his back and looked rather like Santa Claus. "A whole sackful of letters and parcels! The boys will be pleased." He was grinning delightedly.

"Quick, the shortest way!" Jakob told Jan when they were back in the wagon. "I think we could cut off a corner."

"Through Osiny," said Jan, "it will be only half the distance."

"Let's go, then!"

Off they drove through the broad, deserted country, through poverty-stricken villages with mean, straw-roofed huts, through woods and clearings, past reed-ringed pools, and mansions lying in huge gardens behind high walls, on and on, as darkness fell.

Meanwhile, the battery had reached its new quarters. The men were watching out for the long-awaited wagon, but however eagerly they peered into the dusk, there was nothing to be seen. Papa Rosenlöcher was getting quite worked up. "What's become of the lad?"

Cordes laid a fire and lighted the kindling. The White Raven walked back to the crossroads and a little way into the fields. On a slight rise he pulled out the telescope that hung at his belt, put it to his eye, and slowly searched the horizon. There was something moving in the distance, as small as a grain of sand. But the grain grew and grew: there was a wagon out there, drawn by two horses — they were coming!

An hour later the gunners were crowding in line to-ward the steaming cauldron of the field kitchen and each received his portion in his tin bowl.

The mail had been distributed. Lanky Hottenrot had a letter from his wife; Distelmann, with the long beard, had one from his wife and child. Fritz Behr was cutting up a cake that his mother in Bromberg had baked for him and handing out the slices. Rosenlöcher had opened a tin of "First-Class Delicacies" — herrings put up by the firm of Albin Rosenlöcher. He passed one of the tasty fish to Jan, but he was too tired even to eat.

Only when Papa held the herring under his nose and sang, "Cold fish and beet, that's what soldiers eat!", he smiled, his eyes half closed, and took a bite.

Hunger was satisfied. Only the smoke of the soldiers' cigars rose above the weary battery, and soon that, too, disappeared.

In another hour the gunners were lying on the straw, packed tightly together like the herrings in Rosenlöcher's tin, to sleep and dream.

Were they dreams, the dark shadows and dull thuds that penetrated Jan's sleep that night? There was the constant clatter of heavy wagons, the echo of shouts and whipcracks, like the echoes of shots. Once someone trod on his legs, another shook him by the shoulder, shining a torch into his drowsy eyes: "Hey, soldier, what's the way to Osiny?" Osiny? Only half awake, Jan stumbled through the sleeping bodies to the door of the barn in which they lay.

The moon was new and there was scarcely a star in the sky, but on the ground lights moved to and fro, a fire was burning, shadows stood about, and along the roads tramped endless lines of soldiers in grey coats, while broad, heavy wheels turned, groaning on their axles. Jan looked about him, glanced up and pointed to a single twinkling star: "That's the way to Osiny."

Silent shadows and distressful noises broke into his dreams: grey coats, grey faces, grey weapons. Horses coughed, men snored. Once someone cried out, "The war is over!"

But that was only a dream.

❖ INTO THE FIELD

AN KNEW GERMAN, POLISH, AND EVEN A FEW words of Russian. The children in those German settlements all learned these languages as their mother tongue. Often they themselves did not know whether they were using German or Polish words. Now, however, Jan heard a language that was strange to him and much of which he did not understand: the language of the German Army. Many of their expressions sounded familiar, but they had a different meaning, a dangerous and often terrible one. For instance, there was the word *bull's-eye*. Didn't that mean hitting the center when you were playing darts? Wasn't it a matter of celebration? But in military language it has a different meaning: when a shot hits the target in the middle, at the same time destroying all the people there, that's a bull's-eye. When all the shots from a battery are fired at once, that is called a *salvo*. Salvo is a Latin word that means "hail!" but it was a different kind of hail that fell in these salvos. Or "in the field" used to mean a place where you went to sow or harvest; now "going into the field" meant tramping with feet raw from marching and shooting at an enemy you could not see. Jan could not help remembering that among those invisible men called enemies there was his own father. His father was in the field and his father's son was in the field. Why could they not tend the field together as before? Because this field that the soldiers were taking was not a field at all. A real field does not kill, a field lies at peace under God's sun, rain, and wind, a field is where things grow. He had caught the military in a lie. The soldiers were sent into a field of deceit.

Like huge wolves the four cannon of the Seventh Battery went "into the field," across Polish fields, deeper and deeper into Russia, and behind them walked the gunners. Two days, four days, six days, through villages and towns with strange white churches with green roofs, through endless woods, across marshes and rivers. Often Jan thought, it's beautiful, marching like this. The soldiers liked him and they all made a fuss over him. Even the officers were nice to him, and the food was better than at Uncle Peter's. His cheeks grew round again, as they had been when his mother was cooking for him, and his skin tanned. Only the upper half of his forehead, where his cap sat, stayed white, as with all the other soldiers. But they ought not to go on treating him like a child! They themselves looked like children under the caps.

Flox seemed to be enjoying life, too. Skinny Senf with the pointed nose, whose comrades called him Mustard and who had been a saddler before the war, had made the dog a leather collar, and Papa Ro-

senlöcher had sewn a uniform button on it, like the one a lance corporal wears on his collar. Everyone addressed Flox as Lance Corporal Poodle now.

On they went, eight days, ten days, twelve days, and on the thirteenth day it began to rain. Softly at first, then harder, until at last the rain was falling from the sky in sheets.

The autumn storm swept across the endless countryside, driving the rain like gravel into the soldiers' faces until their skin was as sore as if they had been pricked with a thousand needles. The roads they traveled had many a deep hole in them, and the holes soon filled with water to the brim. A child could have drowned in one.

Soon the gunners had not a dry stitch of clothing left. Their boots filled with water and squelched at every step.

The rain fell in their food. The bread, which arrived soaked, was covered with greenish mould, but still they went on. Once they heard that a great battle had been won in France, the war was over. But the war continued, the march continued.

As far as the Vistula.

"A night's sleep!" groaned old Distelmann. "Dry clothes!" growled Mustard, trying to dry his wet face with his wet sleeve. "A bath!" sighed little Behr, scratching himself for the hundredth time.

"Ain't you had enough water yet, you blockhead?" shouted big Hottenrot.

"How long is this going on?" grumbled Lance Corporal Häberlein, when the march stopped and he crept under an ammunition wagon for shelter. "I thought the war went indoors in bad weather."

"My dear fellow," said Mustard, "there'll be no peace till we're in Moscow."

"Then we're in for a bad time! Moscow! Do you have any idea what you're talking about, man?" said Behr. "We'll be like Napoleon."

"What happened to him?" asked Jan.

"Napoleon?" began little Behr. "Never heard of the Emperor Napoleon?"

Jan shook his head.

"He got to the Vistula, too, like us. Crossed the Vistula as well and pushed on — over a hundred years ago, this was — with an army as big as ours. He was going to conquer Russia. He'd already got the other countries, but it wasn't enough for him. So there was an advance — you can imagine it, Panie, just like now — and the Russkis let them march, on and on, just like us. They thought, Russia is big, you can march till you're black in the face. And they retreated, just like now. Napoleon was thinking what a magnificent advance he was making.

"When they were not too far from Moscow, the Russian capital, the snow began to fall — we'll get a taste of that, too. But Napoleon thought nothing of it. He was wearing a big fur coat and traveling in a sledge. There weren't any cars then. But the soldiers were footing it then, just like us, and if anyone wanted to stop, the emperor had him shot.

"When at last they reached Moscow they first set up their quarters properly, dried out their stuff, cooked, and picked off their lice. Napoleon was ready to dictate peace. But there was no one there for him to dictate it to. Somebody'll be along tomorrow, thought Napoleon and lay down for a good sleep. The soldiers pounded their ears, too. They were damned tired, just like us.

"Picture it to yourselves: Moscow is a big city, like Berlin. Just imagine the whole town full of sleeping soldiers — and suddenly, it's burning! They'd set their own capital on fire, those Russkis, and now it was burning from end to end like tinder, because the houses were almost all made of wood."

"I thought it was snowing," Mustard interrupted.

"Oh, well," Behr continued, "it wasn't snowing that night. But all the snow that was still lying on the roofs and streets melted in the fire. Thousands of men were burned to death. The rest ran about like savages, anything to get away from the fire. 'Home' was the password! They got out and ran like the devil, with the Russkis behind them, because suddenly the Russians were there again. That's when they made their advance and chased the Grand Army and the emperor in his thick fur coat and sledge all the way back again. Believe me, Panie, they went back faster than they came. And there was snow again, tons of it. Thousands froze to death and thousands were wounded and thousands were killed. The others ran and ran: all they wanted was to get away from murder and cold, get away! Suddenly they see a bridge ahead of them, crossing the river. They crowd in, pushing forward from behind, more and more of them, and what shall I tell you — Crash! The bridge collapses. Everything on it drowns in the icy water. The ones that followed were shot by the Russians. So what do you think came back to Germany, from all that gigantic army? A few men. And the emperor."

The rain had stopped. The battery halted by a village where they were all hoping to spend the night. They had only stopped because the billeting officers sent on ahead had not yet finished allocating quarters and stables. That was always the way, waiting and waiting. They were used to nothing better: "To sit around and wait — that's the soldier's fate!" Who could tell whether it would be one, two, or five hours — or even half a day. It would not be the first time.

So they squatted on their vehicles, dog-tired, and squeezed together. Some slept, some dozed, some chatted. "What d'you think, Hottenrot," said Papa, "shall we have a game of skat?"

"Want to play, Behr?" said Hottenrot, but Behr wanted to go on thinking about Napoleon.

"Don't be a frog, man," said Rosenlöcher, "you should see the officers in the Eighth Battery — they play all day and half the night! You'd be amazed. They play as much as Captain Tziecke."

"Ziege," Hottenrot corrected him.

"Goat?" asked Jan. (*Ziege* means goat in German.)

"Of course. That's our so-called battalion commander," Behr offered, and Hottenrot explained: "The Goat does absolutely nothing but play cards, booze, and guzzle. Man, I can tell you, the pennies roll where he is."

"It's the old old story," came a voice from under the gun carriage, "Harmless Club!"

"Their skat isn't as harmless as ours," exclaimed Hottenrot, "they play for real money. They lose more in a night than one of us earns in a year. The Czech said there's a report on the way. Seems that the Goat and that Heribert König are winning a bit too much."

"The war is good business for them, but it isn't an honest one," said Rosenlöcher.

"Does the Goat cheat?" asked Mustard.

"He cheats as if he was trained to it, the Czech says," said Rosenlöcher. "Ask him."

And Hottenrot went on, "But when the shooting starts, boy oh boy, does he disappear! You never saw anyone disappear like that. And throw his weight around! It'd take your breath away. He even tries to bully Alert. The Goat — "

"Ssshh!" went Behr, digging Hottenrot in the ribs. A fat-bellied officer with a bloated face came up behind them. "The Goat!" whispered Mustard. Jan had never seen a goat as fat as that, a goat with little piggy eyes. "Talk of the devil," muttered Rosenlöcher. Blown up like a barrage balloon, the Goat headed straight for the gunners and at his side — Jan's jaw dropped — monocle fixed in his smirking face, rode the lieutenant from Gradicz, the one who had struck the horse and whom Jakob had ticked off so smartly.

Jan had jumped to his feet and would have liked to make himself scarce, but the White Raven was already riding up from the other side, which calmed him.

The Goat was close to them now. "What's that snot-nosed brat doing there?" He meant Jan.

"Wearing the Kaiser's uniform, the little devil," jeered König, "a flagrant abuse of Army property."

"Seems a pretty sort of battery," snorted the Goat.

"*My* battery," said Alert, who had heard these last words. "I must ask you, Captain, to present any complaints you may have about my battery to me, the battery commander, or to my superior officer, but not to my men."

"That's my affair," spat the Goat, "and in any case, I won't tolerate your taking boys into the field for your private amusement. I'm giving you an official order: the rascal goes, and that blasted animal, too, that cur, and at once!" Jan was certain that he and Flox would be chased away immediately. Where in the world would they go? He looked up anxiously at Alert, whose face had turned very hard and angry. None of the gunners had seen him look like that before.

"Sir," said the White Raven, "the boy is not going to be sent away. He has served the Seventh Battery and therefore the German Army well and owing to his skill, his goodwill, and — his honesty, he can continue to help us. As far as I know, there is no rule in the German Army against doing a good job, whoever does it. If you think otherwise, sir —"

"Then I forbid it, Lieutenant," bellowed the Goat. "Do you understand? I, your superior officer, forbid it, and that's that. That snot-nosed brat will be sent to a prisoner-of-war camp."

Jan was overcome with terror. But the White Raven looked the wild Goat straight in the eye — just as Jakob had done with the lieutenant, thought Jan — rode up close to him and said, "Forbidden, sir? In the first place, gambling is forbidden, not to mention cheating. I hope you understand me, Captain."

"How dare you?" gasped the Goat, his face turning purple with fury. "I intend to report your monstrous behavior at once. I'll have you before a court-martial." With that he pulled his horse around and shouted over his shoulder: "Seventh and Eighth Batteries advance to Stuszczyn immediately. You'll await further orders there." Then he rode back again, followed by his lieutenant, but Jan thought the balloon was a little deflated.

"He's off his rocker," whispered Rosenlöcher when the officer was out of hearing. "This battery, move on? Now, at night?" Then they heard the shouted order: "Battery ma-a-rch!"

"What a stinking business!" growled Hottenrot, and Mustard added, "The fat man must be off his head. The brute has been chasing us up and down all day and now, in the dark? We'll never make it."

But the wagon train, driven by the command as if by a whip, was already in motion. And it had begun to rain again, harder than ever.

"They can do it to us," said little Behr, and old Distelmann shouted angrily: "But the horses, the poor horses, they're done, completely done. They'll never make it, there's not a chance of them making it. Damned cruelty to animals!"

"Damned slave drivers," said Cordes.

❖ THE DEVIL LEADS
THE BATTERY

NO MAN MUST, NO MAN MUST, UNLESS HE WILL. The words went through Jan's head as he climbed up to join Jakob on the supply wagon. "What about the soldiers, then? Must they, if they don't want to, Corporal?" But Jakob did not feel like talking, and even Birdbeak was no longer chirping. The rain was punishing, and it was so dark that you could not see your hand before your face.

The Eighth Battery was moving in front of the Seventh, and they were scarcely out of the village before the wagon of the Eighth had stuck between two trees. There could be no further advance until the obstacle had been removed. Halt! Shouts and cries rang eerily through the darkness. Men ran about with lanterns and tools, orders were roared out, a saw grated through wood, axe blows resounded, trees crashed to the ground. Then more orders and whipcracks. The drivers shouted, "Get up!" and they moved on.

Jan peered into the darkness, trying to make out recognizable forms. He might just as well have tied a black cloth over his head; the darkness was as thick and solid as pitch, even swallowing up the lights that swung over the cannon. And on top of it all, the rain — that dreadful, monotonous rain! It was a night that weighed horribly on every mind, a night darker than the tomb. A whole sea was pouring down on the earth. It was the night of the Flood. Every minute stretched to an eternity and made everyone still, ready for death.

Now they were moving through a forest, but even the trees were invisible in the darkness. The gunners knew them only by the roots over which they stumbled or fell. The drivers knew them by the twigs that whipped their faces or when a wheel drove into a tree trunk and could not move any further. Then they cupped their hands around their mouths and shouted long-drawn-out commands: "Vanguard h-a-a-a-a-lt!" and the group ahead picked up the cry and passed it on: "Vanguard h-a-a-a-a-lt!" So the word passed right through the Seventh Battery to the Eighth and to the head of the long, long wagon train. Then those at the head halted, but the ones behind did not stop. They could not afford to lose contact, they had to keep up with the vanguard or they would have lost their way. But then the drivers who were stuck and could not move thought they had not been heard and shouted louder and louder and each call was passed up, dully repeated from wagon to wagon: "Vanguard halt! Vanguard halt!" It sounded like the cries of the damned in the grisly darkness.

The horses splashed and squelched through the soft, porridgy mud, which closed up as soon as each hoof was withdrawn.

Suddenly a light flared up: a lurid, terrifying light in the sky, piercing the night like a giant sword, stabbing at the earth, now here, now there. Jan had never seen anything like it. These were the Russian searchlights, searching the whole area for German troops. What if they were to discover the batteries!

Someone asked: "What's the time now?" "Ten," said a voice and then, from quite another direction, "Oh, thanks! What day is it, then?" Silence. Only the wagon wheels creaked and groaned, turning laboriously through the gurgling mud that came up to their axles. And nobody knew that it was Sunday.

Alert ordered the lanterns to be extinguished; otherwise the battery would be discovered by the Russians. Candles must be saved, too. They were already burning the last ends. "It can't be any darker in the grave," said Schnabel.

They crossed a wooden bridge, and beyond it they could just see a small place with a few houses. Suddenly the call came again: "Vanguard h-a-a-a-lt!" It was enough to drive a man mad, but no one spoke. They halted. The silence was sinister. The greenish-white light of the enemy searchlight wandered to and fro. Each time it swept across the battery they could see the rain falling in endless streams.

The last gun crew of the Seventh Battery reported that there was only a single ammunition wagon behind them. The other seven, with the baggage wagons, the smith's wagon, the field kitchen, and the supply wagon on which Jan was traveling with Jakob and Schnabel, had disappeared without trace.

Alert halted his troops and sent back two mounted NCOs to have a look. The rest waited for an hour until they returned, having found no one. To the right they could hear the splashing of the Vistula. Could one wagon have driven into the river in the darkness? But then they would have found the others — or had they been discovered by the enemy searchlights and fallen into the hands of the Russians? Should they give up the search? Should they wait longer?

The situation was hopeless. The long arms of the searchlights reached across the battery, seeming to touch now one cannon, now another. But since the whole train was now standing motionless on the dark road, it went unnoticed. The Russians must have thought they were bushes or mounds of earth.

Utterly exhausted, the gunners leaned on the mud-coated spokes. They were all dizzy with weariness. They cared for nothing now, even if half the battery had been carried away by the rain, drowned in the Vistula, or taken prisoner. "I'd like to flop down in the muck here and rot," said one.

If only the rain would stop! thought Alert, dismounting from his horse. A dog barked in the distance and Alert listened. Could it be . . . the barking seemed to come from the left. It was coming nearer. Could it be Flox? Lance Corporal Poodle? Rubbish, there were other curs in this accursed country. And from the left, too. How could the missing men have got over there? Silence fell again.

But although there was no longer a sound to be

heard, the officer still kept his ears cocked in the direction from which the barking had come.

There it was again! "Flo-o-o-ox!" Alert roared against his cupped hand: "Flooooo-xyyy!"

The barking came nearer and suddenly the dog was leaping up at him, yapping, licking, loving. It was Flox.

For an hour and forty minutes the poodle now took over the leadership of the Seventh Battery. Alert attached a long cord to the collar Mustard had made and put the end into the hands of Sergeant Meumann, the strongest man in the whole battery, remounted, and let Flox go where he liked. For of one thing they were certain, he would want to find his master. In thirty minutes Flox had restored contact with the missing troops and in another hour they were back with the battery.

"Well done, Lance Corporal Poodle. You'll make it to general yet!" said the White Raven, and so saying, he resumed his leadership of the battery.

About midnight they passed through a deserted village. All the houses were empty, doors and windows open, staring like the wide eyes and mouths of monsters at the grey hordes stumbling silently past.

A gunner called Busch suddenly shot out of the line into the darkness.

"What is it? What is it?"

"There! There!" shouted Busch. "There, in the window, that door down there! Russians!" and swinging his carbine to his shoulder he aimed right through the lines of soldiers at an empty, ruined house: "Fire!"

Meumann, the strong man, struck the gun from his hand: "There's no Russians here, man, you're seeing ghosts, you're crazy, man!"

It was enough to send anyone crazy. Jan had fallen off the box when the supply wagon drove into one of the many holes in the road and was now groping his way, drunk with sleep, behind Rosenlöcher through the endless blackness, slipping and sliding at every step. What a misery! Suddenly Papa fell straight into a pit of water and mud, with Jan on top of him. Papa cursed and groaned. His face was covered with muck, his hands torn. And still it rained incessantly, with the same insane monotony.

Another village, equally deserted, and then their way was barred by a stream. They waded through it, the water up ʳo their waists.

Then they turned into a side road that led into a defile which led, steep and straight, into a forest. The gorge was no more than four or five hundred meters in length, but it seemed impossible to surmount. The drivers yelled and whipped the struggling horses, but it was useless. The animals were incapable of taking another step. The battery was stuck. They could not move on and they could not turn, for to right and left of the narrow path the banks rose like walls. In spite of rain, mud, and darkness and their dreadful weariness, they had to go on.

Thirty gunners harnessed themselves to ropes, which were attached to the hubs of the foremost gun carriage wheels, and pulled until their veins bulged.

The drivers beat their horses like madmen. No use.
The gun carriages would not move. They unharnessed
the horses from the second carriage and harnessed them
to the first, still in vain. They took fifty gunners to pull,
still in vain. They harnessed them by tens, still in vain.

With twelve horses and sixty soldiers the heavy gun
carriage was hoisted at last, at last, up the defile. Then
they had to take the teams down again on the treacher-
ous ground. Each time the exhausted men had to hang
on ropes and pull till they had no breath left in their
bodies.

When the gun carriages were up, there were the
eight ammunition wagons to be raised, one after the
other, then the supply wagon, and finally the smithy,
three times heavier than the rest.

They were up, gasping, wheezing, and trembling.
Rest, rest, if only for a moment! But what was this?
From the woods to the left they heard the shouts of
drivers whipping up their horses: "Gee-up, gee-up, ho-
hup!" Just as they had shouted before. This was the
Eighth Battery, which had started off ahead of them
and which they had forgotten in all the confusion and
had lost track of. But it was only a bit of the Eighth:
two gun carriages and nothing else.

"Where is your battery commander?" asked Alert.

"We don't know."

"But where are the rest of the guns?"

"We don't know."

"Your ammunition wagons?"

"We don't know. They're all lost, no matter, good
riddance!"

"And Captain Tziecke?"

"The Goat? The devil take him. He beat it," said the sergeant who was leading the two gun carriages.

"What time is it?"

"Quarter to four."

"Thanks!"

At four the procession crawled on, the men of the Eighth at the back. So the silent, stubborn advance continued.

Tall Hottenrot had stumbled out of line and banged his head against some obstacle, unrecognizable in the darkness. But it enraged him, and he slammed his rifle butt and stamped his feet against the cursed object until it gave way with a loud cracking and crunching. Beams fell, planks split, and the tall man fell forward on the ground. *The ground was dry.* In front of him he saw sparks, white ashes, and a red glow. He was in a spacious barn.

"Häberlein!" he shouted through the entrance. "Cordes! Distelmann!" But instead of the men he was calling, in came Lance Corporal Poodle, shaking himself, and behind him Rosenlöcher, Mustard, Jan, and Behr, also shaking themselves.

They knelt before the feeble glow and blew on it until sparks and ashes flew. A little flame flickered. Flox snuffled and barked. The gunners drew their bayonets, poked up the little fire, and in a moment they had potatoes spitted on the bayonets — hot, wonderful, scorched potatoes. Just as they were going to sink their teeth in them, Lance Corporal Poodle barked again, twice, three times, staring at a corner that contained nothing but a pile of rubbish. "Hush, Lance Corporal!" called Papa, breathing on his potato. But Flox barked again, sharply, as if giving an order. They looked up more attentively. Mustard came over with a flaming brand and saw, among the broken, half-rotted garbage, a tuft of pitch-black hair sticking out. Flox was still barking.

Hottenrot patted him soothingly, tiptoed over to the suspicious pile, grabbed the black topknot, and jerked upward.

"Oo-oo-oo ow-ow!" came a half-stifled howl of pain as the heap took on life and out crawled a ragged, brown man with a scarred face, eyebrows as thick as a moustache, and long, straggling hair. Bent forward, hands high, not looking at the gunners, he hobbled around the outside of the group and made a sudden leap for the door. But Flox and Mustard already had him by the collar. "Bow-wow. You bad gypsy, halt!"

"Haaalt! Halt to the front there!" cried Hottenrot, rushing past the captive gypsy into the darkness. "Halt there!" He had to report their capture.

But those ahead had already halted before Flox had discovered the brown man. The officers had dismounted and were searching the ground with their torches.

The road ahead had disappeared. There was not the slightest trace of any paved way to be found. What now? What to do? The rain streamed down. Then Hottenrot's call, passed on from wagon to wagon, reached the head of the train: "A prisoner, to the left of the eighth wagon, in the barn!" Alert rode off, followed by Sergeant Meumann.

More and more soldiers had come in out of the wet to the dry barn, the potatoes, and the prisoner. They were standing around, chewing, when Alert came in. The gypsy looked up at him, shivering, and Jan felt sorry for the poor devil, remembering when he himself had faced the German soldiers for the first time in Kopchovka.

"Do you understand German?" Alert asked.

"Nix German," he replied.

"Polski?"

"Polski, yes!" The gypsy nodded.

Alert turned to Jan. "Ask him if he can show us the way to Stuszczyn." Jan translated and the gypsy nodded vigorously. "Come on then, he will lead," said Alert. "Shortest way, and at the first attempt to escape he'll be shot. Tell him that, Jan."

Jan did so and the prisoner, guarded by Cordes, hobbled off ahead of the officers. He no longer had any thought of flight. He was only too glad to be still alive.

"Battery, march!"

The long column moved off like a funeral procession across the black, ploughed clods. The gypsy leading them looked like Satan in person.

"The devil!" said a lieutenant, his torch illuminating the dark, scrawny figure hobbling across the furrows in the wavering light. "The devil's leading the Seventh Battery, but where to is anyone's guess!"

"To Hell," came a harsh voice out of the darkness.

❖ A LITTLE CLOUD
OF SHRAPNEL

EVEN THE SHOTS FIRED IN BATTLE CAN HAVE friendly, deceptive names in the language of the military — names that give no hint of the terrible destruction they cause. For instance, when you hear the name grapeshot it's no use thinking of the green or purple grapes bestowed on man by kindly Nature, the sweet fruit of the vine. Grapeshot is something else, a form of shot that scatters, widening the area of the deadly havoc it wreaks.

There is another kind of shot, called shrapnel after its inventor, an English officer. The steel casing contains a large number of musket balls or lead fragments. They usually explode in the air in flight. The white smoke of the explosion gives rise to an attractive little cloud, from which the lead fragments and balls scatter in all directions with a tremendous bang. Just one of these hundreds of fragments is enough to kill a man or to render him an invalid for life.

Jan had now been with the battery for a month. It was October 15. Just as the sun had once pierced the foliage of the birches on the Ravka Bridge, so it now pierced the evening mists of autumn and shone down into a clearing in Stanislovov Forest. The gunners had hung up their soaked clothing to dry between the trunks of the beech and birch trees. They had been here for two days, recovering from the strenuous efforts of the past weeks. They had felled trees and built huts. Each gun and each wagon had its own hut where the men found shelter from the rain and cold. They had even made benches — one for each hut — from the birch branches, on which they sat and smoked, sewed on buttons, greased their boots, and sang:

> *And when the farmer homeward came*
> *The rain had soaked him through,*
> *The rain had soaked him through.*
> *Get up, get up, my beauty,*
> *To light a fire's your duty!*
> *The rain has soaked me throu-ou-ough,*
> *The rain has soaked me through.*

Jan had pulled out his mouth organ and as he did not know the words of the song, he played the melody:

> *But who? But who? But who was guilty —*

"The Goat," Cordes interrupted, "the Goat was guilty!"

The Goat, yes, what had happened to the Goat? Since his clash with the White Raven they had heard nothing of him.

"Hey, Czech, you old lump of dung!" called Hottenrot to one of the soldiers who was just returning with Alert's brown mare and a foal from the stream

where he had been watering the two beautiful crea-
tures. "What's been happening? Did the Goat tattle on
Alert? You're always mucking around the officers with
your long ears — use your tongue now! Did he report
him or didn't he, the coward?"

Czech, a cunning, stocky man with long ears and
bowlegs, grinned scornfully. "Oh, he reported, of
course he reported. What do you think he reported? He
reported sick, that's what he reported, the fat pig. He's
well on his way to Germany now, the cowardly villain.
He's going to have his nerves seen to."

"Instead of to prison," said Cordes.

"Alert's getting the Eighth Battery as well," Czech
revealed in a low voice, "and he's being made commander of half the battalion: Seventh and Eighth Bat
teries. But it's still a secret."

"That's good," said Rosenlöcher, "I'll tell the fellows
at once," and he got up. At that moment there was a
bang above them.

"Papa, what's that?" cried Jan, pointing to the east
where some shrapnel had just exploded.

"Thick air," said Rosenlöcher, "that's just thick air."

"What sort of air?"

"Thick, I tell you, boy, with more bullets in it than
there were beans in the stew tonight. See the flier
there? Just hope he doesn't see us, or we'll be in trouble."

Jan gazed delightedly at the rosy evening sky, against
which the little clouds of shrapnel unfolded like magi-
cal flowers. He could see the flier now, too: tiny, between the little clouds. The dull firing of cannon and

rapid rifle fire echoed from the distance, but Jan did not heed them. He went on staring up at the little white clouds, which were increasing in number. Then something fell from the aeroplane and at once there was a bang ahead, where the firing was coming from. Then everything fell quiet again. The plane vanished.

Eastwards on the Baltic Coast —

sang the gunners,

Stood a gunner at his post,
When a pretty maid came by —

Jan took the harmonica from his mouth. Ahead of them, from the woods, came a strange procession: four soldiers in long, brown coats, with tall, black fur caps on their heads. Their faces were curiously distorted. They were Russians. The song died away.

One had had the skin torn from his cheeks, his left eye was invisible, the right was like a thin line in the swollen, raw flesh.

"Shrapnel wound," said Jürgensen, the medical officer, coming out of one of the huts chewing, and he sent a man for bandages, cotton, and carbolic. The wounded man collapsed, unconscious; the two behind him were dragging on the arms of the German soldiers who had led them in. Jürgensen got out his medical kit. One Russian had his right forearm shattered, the other was bleeding from his left thigh. The doctor, assisted by two orderlies, worked quickly. Jan just heard the words, "Leg's got to come off." Then he moved away, white-faced, unable to take any more. Slowly he returned to the fire his comrades had lit. The fourth Russian was standing there, a dark-skinned giant. In his right hand he was holding a ripped-out plank on which he supported himself as with a crutch. His hand shook, but he stood erect, his teeth biting his lower lip. You could feel that he was in terrible pain, but he stood there as if he felt nothing at all. He did not make a sound. When the doctor came to examine him the Russian turned, flung himself on the ground, touching it with his forehead, and murmured prayers. "Seems to be a Mohammedan," said Behr.

"Mohammedan," Jan repeated. He had never heard the word before, but he was filled with awe at the man's silent suffering.

"Their god's called Allah, and Mohammed is his prophet," Behr explained.

"And they're wretched dogs," said Cordes, "who have the hide taken off them, for the green banner of the Prophet if it's not for the sultan, for Mohammed if it's not for Allah, or little Father Tsar. Allah il Allah, all for the skull of Sultan Mkwawa."

"You mentioned about him once before," said Rosenlöcher. "You was going to tell us about him."

"Shoot!" called Hottenrot.

"Talk, you old mystery monger!" growled Distelmann.

"Get on! Start talking! Tell us!" they all shouted. The Russians were forgotten. Stretcher-bearers had already carried them off to the dressing station. Cordes threw a few billets on the fire. Hottenrot poked at them with a branch, and the fire flared up. The neighboring fires of the other gun crews cast flickering lights. The silence was profound.

"If a lion went and roared," said Rosenlöcher, "I'd turn around and say we was in darkest Africa, having dinner with that there sulky Mkwawa."

"Idiot!" exclaimed Cordes. "Who said anyone was sulky? He's a *sultan,* sort of a chieftain. I expect he was a great ruler, like Charlemagne, or Napoleon, or Barbarossa — "

"Or Struwwelpeter!" Hottenrot interrupted.

"Hold your silly tongue!" said Cordes. "You don't know anything about it. *I* know scarcely anything about it, and I'm a human being!" The gunners laughed.

"It was no laughing matter," Cordes went on, "when the rebellion broke out down there and I was sitting at the trading post with four white men; all the rest were blacks and very uncertain. The medicine men and witch doctors had stirred up the whole country against the whites in the jungles that lay before us. Mkwawa was their talisman, their war cry. Mkwawa gave them courage and such fanaticism that they just ran into our bullets. Naked, with no weapons except bows and arrows, they threw themselves at our machine guns until the corpses in front of the trading post were piled high as hillocks."

"Must be a murdering swine, that Mkwawa," Hottenrot interrupted.

"Mkwawa?" said Cordes. "You probably think I'm crazy, but I'll tell you what was the matter with

Mkwawa: this Mkwawa, for whose sake whole nations were letting themselves be shot to bits, *this Mkwawa doesn't exist.* He may have been a living person once, many, many years ago, when the first white men reached the black continent. In those days — or so a half-mad old woman told me — there was supposed to have been just one gigantic kingdom, and its last ruler was Mkwawa. I don't know if that's true, but the blacks believe it and their witch doctors and ringleaders reinforce their belief. The great chief is supposed to have been killed in the first battles with the whites. His tribe found his mutilated body — without the head.

"His empire soon collapsed into a number of smaller states, which were made subject by the French, English, Belgians, Germans, and so on, and that was when the legend of the skull of Sultan Mkwawa arose among the blacks. If that skull — and no one knows where it is — if that skull returns to his tribe one day, the great ancient kingdom will be reestablished, Africa will chase out all the white people, and the glorious days of Sultan Mkwawa will return. They believe it, and their belief in the skull of Mkwawa is so firmly fixed in the blacks' hard heads that they're prepared to commit any act of folly for his sake. Otherwise they would have left us in peace in our trading post in the end."

"Uhuh, who knows, old boy," Hottenrot teased him. "Didn't you pinch the skull after all? Under the counter, like? When no one was in the shop?"

"You're even more foolish than those blacks," said

Cordes. "If you don't want to listen, just say so!"

"Go on, go on! Shut your dirty mouth, Hottenrot, do you hear?"

"Every minute," Cordes continued, "there was a new assault. The most sleep we ever got was two hours at a time. The rest of the time we sat by the fire on the edge of the plantation, keeping watch. One evening — I was just going to lie down for a bit when an infernal racket broke out. They blew on their buffalo horns, the war drums rattled, they beat their gongs like men possessed and suddenly a horrible yell issued from many thousand throats, and from the blackness of the forest — "

"For heaven's sake, man," cried Distelmann. "Don't tempt Providence!" He had jumped up and was listening intently in the darkness. And sure enough, firing broke out ahead of them, more violently than before, a surprise attack. The crews grabbed their rifles and ran helter-skelter to their cannon, the officers came out of their huts and stood there like helpless children. What could they do? Shooting, but where? Where was the enemy? Or were their own troops firing now? Were the Russians breaking through the front line? If so, they could be here at any moment. *"Tactactactac tactactactac,"* rattled the machine guns, and cannon were now firing from the same direction. Heavy grenades howled over the clearing.

Commands were shouted, the gunners fired salvo after salvo in an earsplitting cannonade.

To the east, ahead of them, an enormous conflagration blazed up. The clouds were tinged with blood.

The savage roar of the cannon rose higher and higher above the clatter of the machine guns. The glare of the fire spread above the treetops, and the black branches reached like ghostly arms into the bloody sky.

What they could see of the fire looked now like a huge monster with red eyes and gaping, fire-spewing mouth. The monster reared up as if seeking its prey, then began to crawl slowly over the wood.

There it slumped down. Had it swallowed up all the uproar of the night? The thunder of the cannon, the hammering of the machine guns — all fell silent. Only an occasional shot could be heard. One of the officers told the men that the Russian push had been beaten back, they could go to sleep.

Later the telephonists reported that the Russians were retreating again, but by that time Jan was asleep.

When morning dawned, the White Raven took the doctor, Captain Jürgensen, Jan, and Flox forward with him. Jürgensen brought along some stretcher-bearers, as well as Jakob and Birdbeak, with whom he intended to shoot some partridge; partridge soup was Jürgensen's speciality. "Partridge soup with noodles and lots of vegetables, that's the best medicine I know," he used to say. He was quite a doctor!

Flox was just as keen on the partridge soup medicine as on the hunt. No pointer could have been sharper off the mark. Now he was swimming across the stream that ran through the old willows to the ditches where the firing had begun the night before. There was a partridge over there that Jürgensen had just shot.

Jan ran eagerly after his poodle. The poodle retrieved and Jan ran to meet him, but as he stooped to take the bird he jumped back in horror. At his feet, arms outstretched and legs spread, lay a Russian. Dead. The half-open eyes gazed straight at him. A drop of blood clung to his right ear. There were many shrapnel fragments on the ground and one in the head of the dead man.

The mists thickened as they walked toward the ditch from which Jürgensen said the fire from the Seventh and Eighth Batteries had driven the Russians the night before. Driven? No, everything was still there: weapons, helmets, caps, and sabers lay in wild confusion on the edges of the ditch; eating implements, clothing, boots, spades, and bloodstained dressings. And in the ditch and in the holes made by the grenades, great God, there they all were. The men were there, brown and grey like the earth and rubble, crumpled or stretched out in dust, blood, and dirt. Men's faces gaped, human trunks stuck out of the ground like tree stumps, human arms and legs lay like hacked branches, human hands and fingers grew out of the earth like plants. This was the field they had dug and planted; this was the harvest that had sprung from the seed of their bullets, filling the whole ditch.

The grave trench was 800 meters long, one meter wide, nearly two meters deep, and full of corpses from one end to the other, in some places right to the top. Jan's eyes flickered to and fro and rested at last, as if seeking help, on one of the many sacred images that lay about, scattered, twisted, besmirched, and that yet gave

to the horror of the battlefield something, a little something of the peace of a graveyard. But this was no
peaceful grave, for not only the dead rested there. Beside and among and beneath the dead lay the men who
still had life in them. They groaned from shattered
jaws, they writhed with mangled and riddled limbs,
they begged their god — after that night of shrapnel
and grenades — for only one gift, death.

But that night, which was simply one night among
thousands in this war, would be dignified in the language of the military by a name: The Battle of Stanislovov.

❖ GOOD-BYE, COMRADE!

THE FIRST SNOW FELL NEXT NIGHT WHEN THE half-battalion moved off at five in the morning it was still dark and bitterly cold. The advance went on, in regulation order: to the front, closest to the enemy, the cavalry, then the infantry, the great mass of foot soldiers with their handguns and machine guns, followed by the artillery with their cannon, and finally the train, the supply wagons. That has been the military order for centuries: cavalry, infantry, artillery, train. The cavalry finds out where the enemy is and reports the route, the infantry marches up and digs in, the artillery fires in great arcs over its own infantry at the enemy troops, hoping to destroy them. After this, the infantry storms in and puts to flight any of the enemy still left after the artillery fire. Those who resist are killed, those who surrender are taken prisoner. This procedure is called a victory.

The Seventeenth Foot Artillery Battalion, known simply as the Seventeenth Foot, marched through the fallow land in light flurries of snow. There came a sudden whistling around the men's ears, like the whine of mos-

quitoes looking for a place to alight and bite: zzzzz-
zzzzz — they all knew that noise only too well. But
where was it coming from? Ahead of them was their
own infantry, as the orders dictated. How could the
Russian infantry suddenly be shooting back here into
the marching column of artillery? Had the German infantry been surrounded? Cut off? Captured? The
enemy bullets were already smashing into the cannons
and gun carriages. If only they could see something!

The firing grew fiercer every moment. From the
front, where the first gun crew marched, came cries,
and then from the second crew, where bullets had
found their mark — on whom, no one yet knew. They
could only hear the screams of pain and each man was
saying to himself: You'll be screaming in a minute,
they'll get you in a minute.

Alert ordered the guns to take up position behind a
copse to the right of the road. They had scarcely
reached it when an officer came galloping up on a
sweat-streaked horse: "Fire! For God's sake, fire!" he
shouted to Alert. "Fire whatever you've got: there!
Over there! Everywhere! We're being surrounded."

"Haven't we got the infantry ahead of us?"

"No, I don't think so."

"So we've no cover at all?"

"None. Shoot, dammit!"

It took the Seventh and Eighth Batteries scarcely two
minutes to get installed: the forepart of the gun carriages, known as limbers, and the baggage wagons were
sent back out of firing range at the gallop, the drivers
whipping up their horses like madmen.

The gunners dragged the shells out of the ammunition wagons. With Jan and Flox, Alert ran straight ahead to a low hillock on which a leafless, bent pear tree was still standing. Two gunners dragged up the heavy steel plate and rammed it into the earth by the tree. Alert and Jan lay down behind it, spying out the land ahead through a hole in the plate. Two more gunners had laid a telephone line, through which Alert issued orders. The batteries began to fire steadily. Jan heard the thunder of the shot, the howling flight of the shells over their lookout post, and then the crash of their landing on the far side of a stream, in low undergrowth. He was listening, his eyes searching sharply from one side to the other.

Suddenly he gave a shout and pointed among the bushes on the near side of the stream, scarcely three hundred meters below their pear tree: "Russians!" Their brown coats stood out clearly against the thin snow. "And there! And on the left! And there on the right!"

The bullets whined more thickly about them; without the shield they would have been lost. Alert shouted his orders and the man on the telephone roared them into the apparatus. At the guns the telephones and gun-crew leaders passed on the commands. The shots thundered over the heads of the observers and fell three hundred meters, then two hundred and fifty, and then two hundred meters ahead of them, in the bushes through which the attackers were steadily approaching.

"Rapid fire!" shouted Alert, following the order immediately with, "Cease firing!" It was madness to go on shooting when the enemy were already so close that the battery could not have helped hitting them in their lookout point as well as the Russians.

"Rifles forward!" roared Alert. "Enemy infantry straight ahead! Occupy the high ground!" And to Jan: "Run, run for your life. The teams must come back with the limbers, the cannon must retreat!"

Jan ran as if the devil were on his back. He could still see the men from the gun crews at a great distance, rushing out of the woods and up the slope, flinging themselves down, getting up again and running on. There was cannon fire from over there, too, now. Jan ran like a madman, Flox always ahead of him, past the gun carriages (only one man had stayed with each, preparing them for departure) over ploughed fields and ditches. Every second was of infinite importance, every second could cost a friend his life.

There — at last — there stood the teams. Jan screamed out Alert's order and on the instant they were rushing, six horses to a team, galloping full-tilt across furrows and obstacles. Jan had swung himself up on the foremost limber and was clinging to it with both hands.

Crash! A grenade struck the ground ahead of them, spattering the team with earth and shrouding it in thick smoke. The horses reared wildly and then galloped on at full stretch through the black cloud. In minutes they were back with their gun crews, to which Alert had by now withdrawn the men on the slopes. In seconds the carriages were limbered up, the drivers roared their "Gee-hup!" and cracked their whips. Gallop! Back! The animals steamed and snorted, the crews ran beside

them, gasping, their tongues hanging out. They took a
field path at the gallop, Jan seated on the third gun carriage. The enemy grenades howled savagely about
them, striking the earth to right and left but no one in
the column was hit. It was a miracle.

Then Czech, the farm boy, came tearing up with
Alert's horses from the right. When he was only eighty
meters from the galloping train, a grenade exploded
right under his horse's hooves. Jan saw through the
spurting mud how the brown mare collapsed at the
knees and fell, a torn bloody heap of flesh. Czech, riding the dun horse, flew over its neck, somersaulted and
lay still, a few meters from the corpse of the brown
mare. Poor Josef Czech.

The dun horse made off in terror, straight into the
enemy fire, and as the gunners rushed to stop him he
fell, pierced by bullets.

Birdbeak, hit in the hip, fell from the driving seat and
was within a hairsbreadth of being run over by the
heavy smithy wagon tearing along behind them. For a
second the man's cry of terror drowned the noise of
flight and bullets. Gunner Busch took a shot through
the shoulder. A grenade splinter struck old Distelmann
in the hand. Sergeant Meumann, the strongest man in
the Seventh Battery, weighing over two hundred
pounds, had his ankle shattered. Horses were hit, too,
which was bad for everyone because the animals shied
and bolted, and the Russians were still firing like men
possessed behind them. They had already reached the
hillock with the pear tree.

All of a sudden someone ahead — it was Driver

Müller of the first gun crew — yelled out: "Swamp!
Swamp! Swamp ahead!" General dismay. The ground
was already giving way under hooves and wheels, the
animals rearing and pressing back. They felt the threat
of the ghastly depths into which they would sink forever. Whips, shouts, even leading by hand did not help,
their instinct was stronger. "They've got to go!" thundered Jürgensen, who had grasped his horse by the bit
and was trying in vain to urge him on. "Set fire to some
straw — when they smell the fire they'll bolt and pull
us through!" The drivers leaped to the supply wagons,
pulled down bundles of hay, and hauled them forward
to set fire to them.

"Why don't you drive round to the left?" asked Jan,
as they ran past him with the bundles.

"Fool!" snorted Driver Müller. "It's all swamp, you
ass. Open your eyes, you damned donkey!"

But Jan and Flox had already jumped down from
their seat. To the left of the road, a stone's throw distant, the tip of an unobtrusive, withered plant was
barely visible above the sparse snow. But Jan had recognized it: it was heather, and as he well knew, heather
never grows in swamps; it needs dry ground. Without
looking back, he ran over to it; he had not been mis-
taken, it was the genuine *Erica*. Flox, who had come
with him, veered off to the right at the clump of
heather. He had put up another partridge and was
going after it.

Two of the gunners had noticed Jan and Flox, and
now Alert saw them, too. Was this a track through the
swamp? Flox rushed off, making a wide arc toward

a distant woodland. The officers followed his every
movement.

"Left turn!" shouted Alert, making it sound like a
cheer.

The whole of the Seventeenth Foot followed the
poodle. In a moment the meadow path was left behind
and they were galloping after the boy and the dog.

"That boy's going to be a general yet," said Jürgensen. He was ashamed that he had been so ready to
waste the good hay. He was a doctor and had studied
botany, but he had not noticed the *Erica* and had almost succeeded in sending two batteries to their death
with his firebrands.

Soon they reached the pine wood, which enfolded
them like a kindly magician, swathing them in its green
cloak where the bullets of the enemy could no longer
find them.

There they threw themselves on the ground and lay
without speaking for at least a quarter of an hour before
moving on again.

But past them, and through their ranks, flowed the
shattered infantry, mindless and in total disorder, rifles
under their arms, bleeding, their wounds sketchily
bandaged, heads hanging, with open collars and tunics,
sunken eyes, and grey-green faces, they stumbled over
the roots, falling from one foot to another. They had no
strength left, even to flee.

The small town of Lutomirsk, which they reached at
last, was teeming with infantry, riders, motorcyclists,
and medical orderlies, a chaos of wounded men, doc-

tors, and stretcher-bearers carrying motionless bodies. The doctors dressed and operated out in the street, to a chorus of groans and cries. Small farm carts were loaded with wounded men and driven off behind the lines.

"Good-bye, my boy," said old Distelmann, his shattered hand in a sling. "Good-bye. I'll have to shake with my left hand, the other's bust."

"Does it hurt a lot?" asked Jan.

"It'll do," said the bearded man, holding his left hand out to the boy. "And thanks, as well. If you hadn't been there with your dog, I'd be at the bottom of the swamp now, me and the whole battery. Good-bye, comrade, and good luck!"

"Say hello to your little Freda from me," Jan called after him.

The little cart into which the old man had been packed with other mutilated men rolled away.

❖ WHY? WHY?

IT WAS AS COLD AS JANUARY, BUT IT WAS STILL OC-
tober. The farmstead from which they wanted to
observe the enemy belonged to a tall, lean man. His
wolfhound beside him, he trudged around his property
as if he were looking for something. When Flox
bounced trustingly up to the strange dog, it growled
and bared its teeth.

It growled again when Jan, Häberlein, and Corporal
Becker fetched a long ladder from the barn, and it
bared its teeth when they climbed onto the roof of the
barn with a telescope. Then the farmer whistled the
dog back and disappeared behind a hedge with it.

In the afternoon Lieutenant Ru took up the watch
with Häberlein and Becker and two soldiers. His name
was really Ruschatzky, but because the name was
much too long for his short figure, Doctor Jürgensen
had abbreviated it on the very first day. Before the war
Ru had been a teacher at the German School in Con-
stantinople, teaching Turkish boys the German language and singing them German songs. Even as a

85

soldier he remained a teacher, giving marks for performance, and he prepared himself for every move as if for a lesson. At that moment he was sitting in the mean little farmhouse with Jan and the telephonist, drawing in the battery observation post and the position of the battalion on his map with a red pencil. Jan watched him. All was quiet outside.

"What do you want to be when you grow up?" asked Ru, putting the map down. "Have you thought about it at all, little Panie?"

In another year I'll be as tall as you, Ru, thought Jan, but he answered, "I'll have to be a farmhand, but if I could choose — "

"What would you do?"

"I'd like to build bridges and embankments for the railways. I've watched the Pioneers doing it. When we were by the Vistula, did you see that jolly one with the red beard? He's an engineer and he's been explaining it all to me. Can he ever draw!"

"Do you like drawing?" asked Ru, but Jan was listening to something else. A heavy shell flew overhead, and they heard it landing.

"We'd better see where that got to," said Ru, and he and Jan went to the door. The shell had fallen some two hundred meters beyond the barn, but the farmer was still strolling about outside. Now he crossed over to the wood.

"Hey, Panie!" called Ru. "You'll get your feet wet. Where are you going?" The farmer seemed not to understand. He glanced back and walked on. Jan repeated the question in Polish, and the man said his dog had got loose, he must look for him. Perhaps he had been frightened by the shot. Jan was startled when he heard the man speak: did everyone in that area speak Polish so harshly? he wondered.

Another thump, as a shell landed behind the hedge. *Boom*, another one: to the right of the barn, the sods of earth spurting almost as high as the barn roof.

"Can you see where they're shooting from, Häberlein?" Ru called up to him. Häberlein shook his head. "Come down, then. No point in getting covered in muck up there. There'll be an accident in the end."

"Weeds don't wither!" said the observer.

"Come down, Gustav," called Jan. "I'll hold the ladder."

Another shot hurtled overhead, landing to the left of the barn, right in the cesspit. Jan was liberally sprayed with manure, and Häberlein laughed loudly from the rooftop: "They're treating Jan with fertilizer to make him grow!"

There was a burst of shrapnel just over the barn and Ru and Jan flung themselves on the ground as the bullets sprayed around them. When they lifted their heads again they saw a soldier lying on his stomach at the foot of the ladder. It was Häberlein. A piece of shrapnel had struck him in the back, and he had slid all the way down the ladder and now lay unconscious on the ground. His telescope was still on the roof, gazing with its long-stalked eye at the horizon.

"We'll have to move the observation post at once,"

said Ru. "I can't understand how the Russians found us here." Becker, the telephonist, pushed an old barrow out of the barn, filled it with straw, and laid Häberlein on it as he painfully regained consciousness.

The Russians were still firing, but that didn't worry Becker. He returned to the barn to bring down the telescope. Ru warned him, "There's plenty of time. Wait till they stop firing." But Becker said, "It's all in our destiny, sir. If God wills, nothing will happen, even if you pass through the heaviest fire. Only please pray, sir. I'll pray, too; down every telephone wire I lay I pray: 'Dear God, don't let this wire be shot to bits and turn the murderous fire away from us and forgive us our trespasses as we forgive our enemies. Lead us back to our beloved homes and deliver us from the worst evil, the war. Amen!' " Almost shouting his prayer, he climbed the rungs of the ladder. Ru was moved by so much trust and courageous simplicity. Becker picked up the telescope and climbed carefully down the ladder while grenades and shrapnel continued to clatter into the courtyard. Now another one hit the barn, but Becker was already on his way to the shed where he had previously put his roll of wire. Heaving it on to his back, he walked calmly to the wagon through the hail of bullets.

He never reached it. He no longer saw the wagon, or the earth itself. The murderous fire had taken both his eyes. He slumped across the shafts of the barrow he himself had fetched and fell on top of Häberlein.

Now he lay on his back beside him in the straw, his

bloody face staring with sightless eyes at the ice-gray sky.

One of the soldiers who had come with the lieutenant pushed the barrow, Jan carried the telescope, and as they approached the wood the farmer, with the dog on its lead, returned. Jan warned him to keep away, but he said, "I'm not afraid." Once again Jan was startled: no Polish farmer talked like that.

Leaving the maimed men with the battery, they climbed a wooded hill to set up a new observation post and then Ru discovered that he had left his maps behind. Oh, God, if they were to fall into the wrong hands! He had had them in the farmer's front room. Jan had seen them there and ran back to fetch them.

As he neared the farm he noticed the farmer standing motionless, looking toward the wooded hill. No, thought Jan, you're no farmer and you're no Pole, either. He hid behind a tree, his eyes never leaving the man.

The "farmer" took a few steps back, pulled a piece of paper from his pocket, wrote something on it, stooped and fastened it to the dog's collar. Then he released the dog, which ran off as if answering someone's call. To the Russians, thought Jan. I must report this to the lieutenant. The dog betrayed us and he's still betraying us. Ru must know, it's more important than the maps. He was already running. Breathlessly he gave his news to the gentle professor, who was instantly like a man transformed. "A spy! I'll put an end to the bastard.

We've still time before his dog gives away our new position. It's lucky I only left the maps and not my army revolver. Come on!"

They made an arc toward the farm, stealing in from the opposite direction. They peered cautiously through a window and saw the man bent over Ru's maps. Lucky the dog isn't there yet, thought Jan. Ru shouted, "Hands up!" The man jumped up, drawing out a pistol, but Ru's revolver barked once. The spy collapsed across the table, his hands gripping the map.

They searched the dead man's body and in a grey oilcloth folder they found some ruble notes and a photograph, a picture of the man himself, with a pretty woman on his arm. He was wearing the uniform of a Russian officer. "There you are," said Ru. "Let's get back to the post, quickly!" And he put the photograph in his pocket.

"You remember this once for all, my lad," said the lieutenant as they walked back through the wood. "A spy is the most dangerous enemy in war. He doesn't fight in the open, he sneaks in, discovers the other side's secrets with cunning and deceit, with theft, lies, and extortion and betrays them for money, for filthy lucre."

"Who gives him the money?" asked Jan.

"The government, the Army Command, the General Staff — there's a special department for espionage."

"Do the Germans have one, too?" asked Jan, startled. Ru nodded.

"The Germans give the villains money — but why? Why do they do it. That's terrible, sir!"

"It is terrible, boy, you're right, but every government does it. As long as wars last, there have been spies and there always will be spies."

Jan was going to say something when one of the men came running toward them from the hill. "Something important?" asked Ru.

"Divisional order," the man reported. "The battery is moving to Willawa."

"Willawa?" Ru spread the creased map out in front of him. "Willawa? Are you sure you heard right? It's umpteen miles to the rear. It's retreat. . . ."

An hour later they learned that the Commander-in-Chief of the Eastern Army, Hindenburg, had given the order for immediate withdrawal.

Why? Why? Why? Why? Again and again Jan asked anyone who would listen, as he sat on the box beside Jakob, driving across the wasted land. Why do the soldiers leave the fields devastated? Why do they let the poor starve? Why don't they work the land and give bread to the hungry? Why do they take the peasants' only cow, their only horse?

"Why did I go and get rheumatism in this damned damp?" demanded Corporal Jakob.

"Damn me," swore Rosenlöcher, "if I'd known before, I'd have hung about at the frontier until you came back. I'd just like to know why they've been chasing us around among the Polacks for three months like loonies: lie down — get up — lie down — get up — forward march, backward march, march! It's worse than basic training. They must be drunk!"

"None of you understand," said Hottenrot, wrapping fresh rags around his feet. "I'll explain it to you. I'm a founder-member of our boxing club, Knockout, at home. We've already won eleven first prizes. Well, war is just like a boxing game. Anyone who doesn't know the art sees nothing but an ordinary fight: one man hits the other, the other hits back, one man ducks, the other ducks, arm in front of his face, bang and the other's got one right in the teeth, so he doesn't know what hit him. Then he goes back on the ropes and suddenly he's off again — no notion why — *bonk*, the other one's got his fist in his belly. There's nosebleeds and faces like footballs and soon one of 'em's down and the other up, whichever. But an expert like me knows what's going on, my boy. There's rules, you know. And it's just the same story in a war. Backward and forward, one hits, they all hit, now they stand and stare at each other, now they walk round and round each other like a circus, and it's all done by the rules. That's science, but you wouldn't know anything about that, that's strategy, but the likes of us have no idea. Strategy is when the boxer makes a plan: first defend, cover up, cover up, until the other man's tired, and then at him like Blücher — there's a winner for you — dead a hundred years ago and we're still remembering how he fought — a straight left to the chin, or the head, or the ribs, that's science, that's called tactics, and it's the same in war. And the likes of us don't know anything about that, either."

"What a wonderful explanation, you old goat," said

Rosenlöcher. "But I knew all that already. Since you're
so fond of wagging your tongue, perhaps you can tell
us, if it's all like a boxing game, then why don't those
gents with their strategy and tactics just get in a boxing
ring and slam each other in their elegant teeth and let
us watch like we was at the pictures? Why do we have
to break our bones for their lousy strategy and bleed till
we haven't a drop left? When we don't understand
nothing about it!"

"Your club may have won eleven prizes all right,"
said Cordes, "but has any of us won a prize yet, ten
thousand or fifty thousand, like a boxer? Oh, yes, a
bullet in the head, a bayonet in the back, or, if you're
very lucky, three fingers gone! I've seen boxing before
now. The boxers shake hands at the end and go off and
have a drink together. Why don't we go and shake the
Russkis by the hand? Because we haven't got any
hands left. No chance of having a drink with a stiff!
Strategy, tactics — the words sound very impressive,
but in good, plain German we're talking about mass
murder and nothing more."

The moon shone down as the battery moved west-
ward, not knowing where. It had all been useless: the
advance to the Vistula, the appalling effort, all the
dead — useless. They heard nothing but the howling of
the wind that cut their faces like knives.

In the morning Jan saw the Pioneers at work behind
the battery. They were the same powerful men whom
he had watched on the advance, throwing bridges

across streams, laying telegraph cables, building supply stores and field railways. Now they had to destroy everything behind them so as not to leave anything of the slightest value for the Russians pursuing the German troops. Not a single telegraph pole was allowed to stand. The torn cables hung from the trees or lay in a confused tangle in the ditch. Even the roads, those wretched Polish roads, were now completely destroyed. Crossroads were alternately left as they were and blown up, until the roads looked like a chess board. Not a wagon or a gun could travel along them now, but trees to the right and left of the smaller roads were cut down to bar the Russians' passage still further. Rails were torn from the ties, switch points smashed, every railway bridge, even the smallest viaduct, blown up with dynamite, and wooden bridges set alight. Every time the gunners crossed one they saw the Pioneers stuffing bundles of straw and barrels of tar under the steps leading to the bridge and between the pillars. As soon as the last man was across the fire blazed up.

"Firebugs! Vandals! Railway saboteurs!" jeered Cordes. "In peacetime you'd all be in prison." There was no answer. Dumbly, with clenched teeth, the Pioneers continued their work of destruction.

By one viaduct Jan saw his friend, the cheery pioneer with the red, pointed beard, but he was no longer cheery.

"That's what you spend your life on," he burst out, "building roads and bridges so people can get to each other easier and quicker and then along comes the war

and you have to destroy them with your own hands.
Have you any idea how much work there is in a bridge
like this! I am not sensitive, boy, really I'm not, but believe me: every time a bridge like this is blown up I feel
as if my own heart was bursting. Why do we work all
our lives? Why?"

❖ NEVER TO MEET AGAIN . . .

I T WAS SUNDAY THE FIRST OF NOVEMBER, ALL
Saint's Day. A uniformed priest went around with a
portable altar and when the troops halted by a forest
he opened it up and held a service before the golden
shrine. Then he spoke to the soldiers, of their dead
friends and the sufferings of the wounded. In the middle of his sermon it began to rain, as if Heaven itself
were weeping for the war and those who had abused
God's commandment.

"But sunshine comes after rain," the priest consoled
them. "Anyone who gets home alive and well after this
war has been preserved by God for great things. This
war will be the last of all wars. That's what we pray
for, that's what we're fighting for, it's for that that our
comrades fell. Your sacrifices will not have been in
vain."

After he had spoken the benediction, he added,
"There's one bit of good news in store for us all: some-
time tomorrow you'll be crossing the frontier. We'll see
Germany again!"

Germany! The word shot like lightning through the

batteries, battalions, and regiments, filling all the men with inexpressible joy. Germany, their mothers and fathers, their children, their brothers and sisters, homes, and jobs! Just to say the word was like a great inspiration of breath: *Germany.*

The battered feet, the frozen toes suddenly didn't hurt anymore; they walked behind the cannon of their own volition, and the men's hearts beat out the rhythm: home again, home again, home again! Now, even when they were awake, they dreamed of home. The song that had been on their lips when they set out three months before, cheerful and unsuspecting, rang out again as they climbed aboard the train that was to carry them over the last stretch to the frontier and across, the song of a soldier's homesickness, with the recurring chorus:

> *In our homeland, in our homeland,*
> *That's where we'll meet again . . .*

They roared it out again and again, until the whole train was singing: "In our homeland, in our homeland. . . ." Only Cordes sang, ". . . we'll never meet again . . ."

The others crowded to the windows: "Are we at the frontier yet? How far is it now? Why does this bloody train go so slow?"

"I'll get out and help push," said Rosenlöcher.

The stations they passed through still had foreign-sounding Russian names: Dembricze, Skrzunki, Zawady, Podgrabow — then at last: "Hurrah! Hurrah! Hurrah!" A frontier post, painted black and white, the Prussian colors. And a stationmaster with a red cap, and then, "Hurrah!" roared the whole compartment: a letter box, a proper, fat, blue letter box! "Hey, look there!" crowed Papa, his eyes moist. "See the blue postbox, Panie? German post office, do you know what that is?"

"Look what's written there, my son!" Hottenrot tugged him to the window on the other side. "Halt when the gates are down! You can *read* something like that, it's a language a man can understand, that. They don't have anything like that in the whole of Russia."

"Odol, best for the teeth," shouted Driver Müller enthusiastically. "Can you read, little Panie: it's Germany!"

They rollicked and reveled as if they had been drinking, singing at the tops of their voices:

> *Swing the banners to the sky*
> *Over the battalion high,*
> *Swing them high above our corps*
> *Heavy guns are to the fore.*

In their joy they saw themselves as conquering heroes coming home. Everything they saw was new and glorious in their eyes.

"Look there, Lance Corporal Poodle," cried Mustard, pointing to the forest to the left of the track, "that's a bit different from the dirty old Russian jungle with all that wailing and gnashing of teeth! A wood like that's a sheer pleasure. It's got a few empty tins in it and some wrapping paper. It's like being home with mother, lad."

"And look at that pavement, son!" babbled Rosenlöcher. "You could eat your dinner off it and not pick up a spot of dirt."

"*Girls,*" they suddenly all shouted at once, crowding to the left-hand windows and climbing on the seats, goggling and waving and shouting: "Marie! Lisbeth! Anna! Katie! Mousey! Sweetie!" The girls giggled and the gunners swung their caps and sang:

> *Come, lass, don't look sad,*
> *Life's not too bad,*
> *Don't make your poor gunner's heart stop . . .*

The train moved on, the song died away:

> *You know this campaign*
> *Is no express train,*
> *So wipe up your tears with a mop!*

"Say, Cordes, you haven't opened your trap, you lazy dog," said Rosenlöcher, shaking his friend, who sat there unmoved by all the fuss.

"I don't want to spoil your pleasure, children," said Cordes.

"What's up with you then — not enjoying yourself, old Mkwawa?"

"Oh, yes, Mkwawa," said Cordes. "Now you're getting all excited over his skull again, and I can't join in that."

"But there ain't no skull, that's what you said — no one can find it. This here is Germany, you can see that. We're back home in Germany, get it?"

"Really?" said Cordes. "Home in Germany? All I

can see is a pair of black-and-white-striped posts and blue letter boxes. What else? Those girls back there, they were Polish. You could have seen that from their colored kerchiefs, and what about the places? We went from Podgrabow to Grabow, then we stopped in Wiclowicz, the girls were at Sicriszcewice, and now we're coming to Ostrowo. Doesn't sound much like home, does it?"

"You don't understand, old man," said Rosenlöcher. "This is *German* Poland."

"And all that time we were in Russian Poland. Poland is Poland, so you tell me, what are you fighting for? What are you getting so excited about?"

"Germany."

"No, just about the color of some posts and some letter boxes — that means even less than the skull of an African chief."

When they reached Ostrowo, little Behr saw Jakob walking up the platform. "Corporal," he called, "Corporal, can you tell us if we'll be going through Breslau, or is it a secret?"

"No idea," said Jakob, "but wait a minute, I'll see if Ru knows something."

But Ru knew nothing, or else he pretended not to, for all troop movements, whether at home or abroad, were kept strictly secret for fear of spies.

"What a dirty trick!" snorted Driver Müller, getting back into the compartment. "We'll be unloaded like a herd of cattle and no idea where we're going."

"To the slaughter," suggested Cordes.

Beyond Ostrowo the train changed direction and began to travel north. Behr noted it on his compass. "So we're not going to reach Breslau in this life," he said.

All of them stared wordlessly at the compass, and their hearts began to quiver like the small black needle that was still showing them traveling north.

Suddenly Behr clutched his head: "We must have been crazy not to have figured it out! Did you see the names? We're going to occupy the coast — "

"Stop your noise and don't scare the horses!" said Corporal Skobel, one of the new ones. "Danzig, Neufahrwasser, Pillau, that's where our so-called active batteries are deployed in coastal defense."

"That's it, that's it," rejoiced Behr, "we're going to relieve them. They've been loafing about long enough. Now they're for the Russkis, and we're going to drink Danziger Goldwasser and eat crab and catch shrimps. . . ."

". . . Yes, when there's a blue moon," came a comfortable voice from Rosenlöcher's corner. "And I'm going to have a bit of a snooze. You can wake me when you see the sea. Good night."

" 'Night, Papa!"

Next morning the train crossed a bridge and stopped. The men scrambled down the railway embankment to the river, where they washed. Papa was the first to notice the signpost. Still wet, his chest bare, he ran over to it. His face cleared. "Cordes!" he called. "Hottenrot, Müller, Panie!" They went to him. "If that isn't German, I'm a Chinaman," cried Rosenlöcher. On the signpost they saw: Ganshagen 4 km — Neustadt 6 km. "Do you believe in home now, Mkwawa?"

But before Cordes could answer came the order: "Detrain! Half-battalion to march to Szczodrzejewo."

"Szczodr . . . for Heaven's sake, you can't pronounce it at all."

"Sneeze three times, spit twice, and you've got it," said Hottenrot, spitting on his hands and grasping the wheels of the third gun carriage. "Hoooh-hup-hooohhup!"

"Is that in Germany?" groaned Rosenlöcher, when they had unloaded the wagons and the guns. Ru said it was. From the place with the unpronounceable name to the border was a distance of 6 km.

And off they marched. That same afternoon they were back at the border.

Rosenlöcher stood by the frontier post. No one noticed him. He felt as if he could not take another step. Overcome by a sudden weakness, he leaned against the black-and-white-striped post, staring back hopelessly toward Germany. His cheeks were drawn, his lips blue. He looked as if he were going to collapse.

"Rosenlöcher, come on! What's the matter with you?" came the voice of a sergeant from far away.

"Papa!" called Jan.

The old gunner pulled himself together and trotted forward until he caught up with his unit.

❖ DOMBIE

OF THE ORIGINAL ONE HUNDRED AND SEVEN-
teen horses in the battery, only eighty-two
were still alive. Of the two hundred and fifty
gunners, ninety-six were dead, wounded, or sick. Eight
of the wounded were awarded the Iron Cross, but this
distinction gave them no pleasure. On the day before
the medal arrived, Sergeant Karl Meumann, the strongest man in the Seventh Battery, had had his foot amputated on the operating table of the reserve hospital.
Gustav Häberlein lay on the next floor up, encased in
plaster, with a high temperature. Blind Johannes
Becker felt the black-and-white cross with his fingers in
an institute for the blind and said not a word. Then he
dropped it and picked up a wooden board that lay before him on the table. He was learning Braille.

But the gaps made in the ranks of the battery by ill-
ness, wounds, and death were filled up again. Wherever
they came across a horse they took it and gave the
owners a receipt: Received, 1 horse. Signature . . . This
was called requisitioning, and they requisitioned
everywhere they could and everything they needed.

103

There was a wretched hut consisting of only two rooms, one where a family lived and slept and a stable. In the stable was the family's only horse, a fine, powerful grey. They had hidden it there and walled up the entrance, for it was their one possession and they all loved it. Through all the weeks, while the Russians, the Germans, then the Russians again, and now the Germans again, moved through the place, they tipped the horse's fodder in from above, through a hole in the attic, and lowered its water in a bucket by rope to keep the horse from being requisitioned.

But it struck Driver Müller that the room he had staggered into was much smaller than the little house — and there was no door, either inside or out — to the unexplained space. There was not even a window. Had they got weapons hidden there, spies, enemies?

He reported his remarkable discovery and Lieutenant von Allenstetten came at once and ordered the wall to be broken down. Then he wrote a requisition order and with Corporal Skobel and Driver Müller rode out of the farmyard with the grey. But the owners, an old peasant, his wife, two grown-up daughters, and a boy of Jan's age knelt before the officer, crying, wailing, and begging. It was enough to break your heart. They kissed the hem of his tunic, they clutched his legs and kissed his muddy boots, they raised their eyes to Allenstetten's face and prayed to him as if he were God. But he was not God, he was a soldier and soldiers are cruel. "The horse no longer belongs to you. Here is your receipt for it," he said, and left. Their crying turned to despairing shrieks, to convulsive sobs; they threw themselves in his path and kissed the earth beneath his feet, in vain.

"Why did you do that, sir?" asked Jan, who had watched the whole event in silence.

"I'm sorry," Allenstetten replied. "Regulations. The people were given a proper receipt."

"But they can't harness the receipt to the plough," said Jan sadly.

Soon after that, Lieutenant von Allenstetten was promoted to first lieutenant and commander of the Seventh Battery. Some of the men and noncommissioned officers were also promoted and some received the Iron Cross. Cordes and Hottenrot became lance corporals. Hottenrot thought a lot of himself, and his tongue wagged even harder than before. Little Behr became a corporal, and took over poor Häberlein's job as observer. Jakob became a sergeant; Alert was promoted to captain and was awarded the Iron Cross First Class. The new divisional commander, General von der Aue, pinned it on Captain Alert himself, in the great market square in Kolo, where the troops were drawn up for inspection. Jan was there, too, and heard the general's speech, but although he was standing quite near the front and von der Aue spoke very loudly, he did not understand much of the long discourse. The powerful voice spoke of laurels, fame, the flag, the fatherland. And the importance of holding out.

"Holding out. How do you do that?" Jan whispered to Lance Corporal Cordes, standing beside him.

"Holding tight, holding your tongue, and holding the fort, that's holding out," said Cordes. Jan grinned. "And what — " He was going to ask what are laurels, when he got a sharp look from the divisional commander. The sentence stuck in his throat and he thought: hold your tongue!

When the speech and the distribution of the Iron Crosses were over, Alert was called to the divisional commander.

"Captain," said the general, "in the last few weeks you and your troops have excelled yourselves, yes, excelled yourselves. Accordingly I am not going to take the matter on which I have summoned you here very seriously. The division headquarters recently received a report, an unsigned letter, but containing very specific allegations which, if true, would severely incriminate you."

"A denunciation, in other words. May I ask Your Excellency to inform me of the contents of the denunciation?"

"I took it for granted," the general continued, "that it was libelous. You have been accused of putting an underage prisoner in Prussian uniform instead of handing him over according to the regulations and, in spite of the danger of espionage, involving him in military service. As I said, I did not believe it, but just now I caught sight of a lad in the Seventh Battery. The rascal had the impudence to laugh. Is that the boy?"

"If it please Your Excellency, that is the boy. It's the same boy who brought back seven lost munition wagons during the advance on the Vistula. It's the same boy who brought the gun crews back under heavy shrapnel and grenade fire and, thanks to outstanding observation, saved the half-battalion from drowning in the swamp. It's the same boy, Excellency, who unmasked a Russian officer disguised as a spy only a few days ago. I must confess, Your Excellency, that I wear this distinction," he pointed to the decoration on his chest, "which I received a few minutes ago from your own hands, with some shame because it's only there thanks to that boy. Without him there would not be a single man of the Seventh or a single man of the Eighth Battery standing in Kolo marketplace today."

The general's face had grown more kindly as the White Raven spoke. "I was young once, Captain Alert," he said at last. "I'm convinced of the boy's soundness and of the integrity of your intentions, my dear fellow. But officially I may know nothing about the matter. The story must on no account get around, you understand, or we'd be in the soup. Think of it: the Germans are kidnapping minors and misusing them for dangerous service! That's how it would go, you may depend upon it. That's how they'd take it in both enemy and neutral countries, and what would be the consequences? This damned letter claims that the boy is a Russian national. If that were known, our enemies would take countermeasures, they would practice retaliation and would put German children in the trenches as soon as they were captured. Have you thought of that, my dear Alert? No. So that's all I have to say. You do what you think right, but I don't want to see the boy again under any conditions."

Alert could well imagine who had written that letter: the Goat or Heribert König — probably the two together. It made him all the less inclined to send little Panie away to a prisoner-of-war camp in payment for all his courage and capability. Even Ru and Allenstetten would not hear of it when he discussed the matter with them. "As long as the Old Man doesn't see the boy, everything's in order. That's all he wants," said Allenstetten. "It's simple: we'll just hide the kid when a general's coming."

And that was the beginning of a game of hide-and-seek in which the half-battalion took part with enthusiasm. They were not going to have their Panie taken from them. "If they take you away, my boy," said Rosenlöcher, "I'll not play along with them no more, they can strike me dead."

"So, listen," said Jakob, "whenever you see one of those officers with a broad red stripe on his trousers — that's what all the generals have so you can see them a long way off — make yourself small and come to the forage wagon. We'll throw a tarpaulin over you and no one will see you. No one gets into my forage wagon that easily."

The White Raven found all this secrecy distasteful. He could no longer take Jan with him openly, and he did not want to take him in secret. But he needed him, especially for observation. Jan saw more with his naked eyes than the rest did with telescopes. The boy seemed to have a feeling for anything that was not quite right about the landscape; no matter how well the Russians hid their observation posts, Jan found them, because in some way they had altered and distorted the natural conditions. A treetop that did not bend to the wind with the other branches, a black point interrupting the gentle line of a hill, a trampled patch of ground, the flight of startled pigeons from a house roof or of a hare in a field, all these things told him where a man might be hidden, disturbing the peace of nature.

Now Jan had to stay with the guns while Alert went forward on reconnaissance with Ru, Behr, and the telephonist. The Russian guns were already thundering and Alert's orders came down the wire for the Seventh and Eighth to fire, first individually, then in salvoes.

"That could be expensive," said stout Dambach, who had been an insurance agent. Rosenlöcher patted him on the stomach. "You'll get quite slim in the end, old tub; look at my trousers. They used to be too tight, and now I could get into them twice!" Then came the command: "Rapid fire!" and they could no longer hear themselves speak.

Suddenly no more orders were coming through from the front. The telephone rang, but the observation post didn't answer. Had the telephone cable been hit, or had something happened to the officers? Before anyone in the battery could decide what to do, Jan had taken off through the forest.

The heavy German shells flew howling and grumbling from the Germans behind and the Russians ahead of him. It was almost like the day when he had first experienced the horrors of loneliness under fire, in Kopchovka on September the fourteenth. But in the two months since that day, he had gained enough experi-

✦

ence to know how to throw himself down when a shell was on its way and to recognize from the sound whether it was going to drop close by or scream past. He knew better than many soldiers, and moreover he now had a goal, a job to do: he wanted to help people who had been kind to him.

If the Russians are moving in on them the way they did when we were by the pear tree behind the steel shield, he thought as he ran, Behr won't see them! By the time he's wiped his glasses he'll be shot, and the White Raven, too.

He kept his eyes on the telephone cable that the telephonist had unrolled behind him when he went off with the captain two hours earlier. From time to time Jan gave it a tug to see if it was still firm — and at last it gave way. Thank God — now he knew! He had the torn end in his hand.

He soon found the other end, broken off by a tree as it fell. Could he possibly put the two ends together properly? He had thoughtfully provided himself with insulating tape and a spare piece of cable, and he had watched the telephonists mending torn cables before now. It shouldn't be too difficult. The penknife Papa had given him had a powerful blade, too, so now, to work!

He no longer heard the howling of the heavy shells, or the firing and explosions. He was completely absorbed in his work.

There, it would hold now, but would the line still work? He listened tensely the next time the cannon fired and observed where the shells were traveling.

Right, they were no longer speeding straight ahead as before — they had moved a good way to the right. That would not have been possible without an order from Alert, so he must have been able to speak to the battery.

Should he return to the guns? By his reckoning there should already be technicians on the way, searching for the break. They were going to get a surprise, finding the cable already mended! Should he wait for them here? It would be fun to see their astonished faces!

But there was an uneasiness that would not leave him, driving him on through the forest, his eyes still on the cable.

He was through the forest and could now see three wooden posts some distance away. Behind one of them, to the right, he could see prone figures — those must be his officers. But the shells were falling between the posts. Fir trees were splitting and collapsing. The Russians were shelling the edge of the forest.

Now the German shells were howling high above him, across the level ground in front of him. At the edge of the ground, to the right of the hill to which a roadway led, lay a town, the target of the battery's shells. Where they fell, fires broke out.

First a barn to the right caught fire, then a house to the left, now one in the middle. Then the shells and the fires followed one another so fast that soon the whole town was one vast flame, and from the flames rose a thick, blackish smoke, which curled back on itself before rising in a giant pillar toward the sky.

Jan turned his eyes away from the work of destruction. A stream running out of the wood twisted and turned ahead of him. The little boys from the town would have bathed there on summer evenings. What would become of them now, without house or home? He was well off, his home was the battery.

On the far side of the stream, among sparse bushes, there were some small houses, shepherds' huts and peasants' cottages. Above one of them the air shimmered as it would normally do only on a hot summer evening. What could that be? Did it come from the burning town? Jan wetted his index finger and stuck it in the air: the side of his finger toward the wood was cool, so the wind was coming from there, not from the town. Or was there a fire inside the house, was it inhabited? If so, he was sorry for the poor people inside, who might be struck by a shell at any moment. But there was no smoke to be seen, however hard he stared at the chimney. What could it be? He thought hard, but then from behind, from the forest and to the right on both sides of the road, the infantry came marching up.

Soldiers ran forward in long rows with wide spaces between them, flung themselves on the ground, were followed by a second line, which ran through the prone figures and themselves lay down some forty or fifty meters ahead of them. Then the first row jumped up again and threw themselves down as a third came out, and so on, like the waves of the sea — or like moths, flying ceaselessly into the flames on a summer's night: the grey soldiers, driven by an invisible force, ran toward the burning town, toward close fighting with the Russian infantry waiting there for them.

But before the first line reached their goal, machine

guns were chattering: *tactactactac — tactactactac tactactac*. Soldiers fell, out of their ordered rows, on their backs, on their faces, or stumbling forward a few paces before collapsing, but still fresh human waves broke over them and the machine guns rattled out their merciless fire: *tactactactac tactactactac*.

Suddenly Jan knew what the shimmering air above that lonely house meant. All at once it was clear to him: there was a charcoal fire in there, and charcoal gave no smoke. Beside that fire the men had been sitting, waiting, lying in ambush until it was time to slaughter.

His friends with their horn-rimmed glasses and binocular telescope had not seen this, and he must tell them at once. He crawled over the trunks barring his way, hid in the crowns of fallen trees, and at last reached the second woodpile. If only they couldn't see him from across the way now. He had no more cover, he would have to return to the protection of the brushwood at the edge of the forest. The bullets mustn't find him, not now, not until he had pointed out that house of death to the White Raven!

"The fourth house from the right, from the road!" he shouted to Alert. "There, yes there, machine guns, fire, Captain, fire!"

"Seventh Battery, concentrated fire!" shouted Alert, after sending a new order down the telephone. Without thinking it over, simply in obedience to instinct, the instinct of trust and total reliance aroused in him by the young voice, he aimed the four cannon of the Seventh at the house, using two cannon of the Eighth on each of the neighboring houses: *direct hit*. The machine guns fell silent and the lines of infantry stormed on into the heart of the burning town.

The guns were silent, but from the level ground on either side of the stream, to right and left of the road, came long-drawn-out cries of pain, cries for help, whimpering, groaning, and more cries. Orderlies ran forward with stretchers and dressings in boxes with a red cross painted on them. But what could their few hands do against the mountain of suffering growing up out of the ground?

The observers stood up. "That brave lad," said Alert, "has saved thousands of lives."

"Without him the assault could easily have failed," said Ru. "I kept thinking of the Maid of Orleans. Didn't you think of that, too?"

"How can I thank him?" asked the White Raven, looking around. "Jan! Hey, Jan!"

But Jan had made himself scarce. He was back with the guns, now advancing along the highway.

The gunners now saw the burning town. "Was that our work?" asked Cordes.

"What else?" said gunlayer Corporal Skobel. "Where I've laid my gun the grass doesn't grow again. Every shot a direct hit."

"What's the name of the town, Corporal?"

"Don't know."

Cordes turned to Sergeant Dietrich: "Can you tell me the name of the town we've set alight, Sergeant?"

"Doesn't matter to me, much less to you."

"Just as you say, Sergeant."

As they approached the first of the smoldering houses, Cordes said to Jan, who was walking beside him, "At least an arsonist knows what he's burning."

The battery drove through the town, which was still smoldering everywhere. Bare walls reared up, black and charred. Behind the cavernous windows flames blew like curtains. The little market square was full of straw, and the straw was red and wet with blood.

Now they turned into a narrow street. The houses on both sides were smoking. The gutters on either side of the steep little street ran with blood. The dead lay all over the roadway, Russians and Germans. This was where close combat with knives and side arms had raged most furiously.

It was impossible to get the corpses out of the way, impossible to go around them, hemmed in by the burning houses. The horses became uneasy and stepped delicately across the bodies, but the wheels of the gun carriages moved forward horribly over crunching bones. Forward, forward!

"Cordes," said Jan, "I'm going to be sick." His voice sounded like an adult's, his face was greenish-yellow. "Give me a cigarette, Cordes!"

Cordes handed him one and lit it from his own.

Jan smoked for the first time in his life.

Flox slunk behind his master, his tail between his legs, careful never to touch a dead man with his paws. Suddenly he began to whine. "Come on, Flox, poor boy!" called Jan, but the dog had stopped. He was standing beside a Russian soldier lying against a wall with his legs drawn up. The dog was licking his hands, whining more piteously, almost as if he were crying.

"What's the matter with him?" asked Cordes.

"Flox, what is it?" asked Jan and turned back to look at the dog. Instead, he saw the face of the man — oh God, where had he seen that face before? He knew it, contorted and smudged as it was, he knew it. It was — who was it? The fallen man's eyes had been fixed rigidly on Flox, but now he raised them to Jan and now Jan knew who it was: Vladimir, the shepherd who had worked for their landowner, Vladimir from Kopchovka, Flox's master. Now he lay dying and his dog tried to lick his cheeks, but his head lolled to and fro and his mouth hung open.

Jan tried to give him his lighted cigarette, putting it between the man's teeth, but Vladimir's head went on shaking, and the cigarette fell in the gutter, to be extinguished in blood.

"Water?" asked Jan. Vladimir still shook his head. He raised his right hand, its index finger pointing to something black that lay between him and the wall. Jan picked it up: a New Testament in German, besmirched and bloody. Between its leaves lay a postcard.

The shepherd's body fell slackly to one side, his jaw dropped. Jan stood as if lifeless, the black book still in his hand.

Cordes laid his arm across the boy's shoulders. "Nothing to be done, he's dead now. Did you know him?"

Jan's thoughts were far away. He could see Vladimir,

in his black, matted sheepskin, in the meadow with the sheep . . . when one was sick he cured it, oh, Vladimir knew about animals . . . he could see Vladimir in his new uniform, going off to war across the Ravka Bridge with Jan's own father. He could see them waving —

"Is he from your village?" asked Cordes. Jan nodded. "Come, I'll carry him to the side so that the wheels don't — want another cigarette?" Jan shook his head.

The battery halted in a field behind the town. Jan and Cordes had rejoined the others.

Allenstetten had dismounted and was marking something on his map. Cordes went over to him. "Excuse me, sir, may I ask the name of the town we've just come through?"

"Dombie," said the lieutenant. "Why do you ask?"

"I want to make a note of it," said Cordes. "Dombie. I shall remember that name all my life."

"Good, Lance Corporal Cordes. The Battle of Dombie is a glorious chapter in the history of this campaign. We can all be proud of it," said the officer.

❖ ADVENT

IN THE ARMY EVERYONE WEARS A UNIFORM — EV-
eryone, from simple gunners and infantrymen to
generals and field marshals. The word *uniform*
means equal, alike all over, but like so many military
words this word, too, is something of a deception.
Speaking plainly: it is a lie.

Firstly, the uniforms of generals and officers are of
finer cloth than those of the men. You can see that at
first glance. They are made to order and they fit well,
even the boots, which are of the finest leather. Whereas
the uniforms of the men are clumsy-looking, mass-
produced — and if a pair of boots really fits, it's a miracle.

Secondly, all the uniforms, from lance corporal on up,
have special badges or insignia on the collar, shoulders,
cap, sleeves, and even on the trousers. These make the
"uniform" into an expression of boundless inequality
and dissimilarity. The soldier is bound, under pain of
severe punishment, to salute these sewn-on insignia,
woven stripes, stars, buttons, colored flashes, and so on
with the greatest respect, just as William Tell, the lib-
erator of Switzerland, had to salute the hat of the tyrant

Gessler. But Tell, a free man, would not salute and became a hero. As soon as a man puts on a uniform he is
no longer free. Is he still a man? Not in war. In war he
becomes a killing machine and the officer, whether he
likes it or not, becomes the killing machinist. The infantry serves mostly as cannon fodder.

Cannon fodder — one of the most horrible expressions in the language! It does not refer to the oil used to
grease the cannon or the shells pushed into their insa-
tiable barrels; it means *people*, driven before the cannon
by tyrants who feed their hunger.

A man with stripes on his uniform is called "superior." A man without stripes, or with fewer stripes, is
called "subordinate." The simple soldier is also called
"common," although he is no commoner than his superior with the fancy title of noncommissioned officer, officer, or staff officer. Even a soldier of forty or more, like
Distelmann or Rosenlöcher, for example, if he sees
someone coming toward him wearing an insignia,
someone he has never seen before, someone young
enough to be his son, then Distelmann or Rosenlöcher
has to greet him, not with a pleasant "Hello, how are
you?" Oh no. At least six paces before they draw level
he must straighten his body, snap his right hand to his
forehead, tick-tock! and stalk past the decorated young
gentleman as stiff as a broomstick. Only when he is
three paces beyond him can he start walking like a
human being again. In those days even the cars that officers used had to be saluted, and even if there was no
one sitting in them — empty cars!

All this happens in the name of military discipline, to

which ordinary common sense and human freedom are sacrificed. In the military, discipline means that each man has to do what his immediate superior tells him to do. This superior must do what the next-higher superior commands. No one may contradict his superior, for contradiction and free discussion, however justified, is the worst crime. It goes against discipline. And if the command sends the soldiers to certain death, the soldiers are not allowed to grouse.

Late at night on the fourth day of Advent, after long, hard, and bloody battles at Lutomirsk and Kasimirsk, at which forty-two men of the Seventh and Eighth Batteries met their death, the Seventeenth Foot was once again loaded onto a train.

Dreadful days lay behind them: among the dead of Kasimirsk was little Fritz Behr, who was on forward reconnaissance and was just polishing his glasses in order to observe better when he received a direct hit that killed both him and the telephonist. They found only his pack, containing his diary, which was sent to his mother. It contained a few poems as well, the last entitled "Advent."

Lieutenant Ru also kept a war diary, in which he noted all the important events and made comments on them. While the gunners were loading the cannon and gun carriages onto the train, he was sitting on the loading ramp making the following entry: "Behavior of troops: good. Memory: faulty. They are scarcely out of the mud when it is all forgotten. It's the same with me.

You shake the horrors off you, like Flox shaking the water off him when he's wet. If men were not so terribly forgetful, there would be no more war."

The train on which they were to be moved was endless. Behind the engine was a second-class coach for the officers with boards hanging on the outside inscribed: Staff. One compartment was for Alert, the other for Ru and the doctor. They were generously heated. The officers took their coats off and made themselves comfortable.

The men traveled in cattle cars, which were less comfortable. There were no padded seats — in fact, there were no seats at all, nor was there any heating. The last three cattle cars were filled with the sick and wounded from a field hospital, but as they were attached at the end of the train, behind the guns, the doctor could have a peaceful afternoon's sleep without being disturbed by the groans of the sick and the moans of the wounded, while Alert stretched his legs in the corridor.

"Why don't they put the poor fellows in the carriages with the padded seats?" Jan asked Dambach, the insurance agent.

"Because," said the fat man, "an officer's rear is worth more than the worthiest of us ordinary mortals."

Jan looked out over the wide Polish countryside, which had been his home and which he was now leaving again.

It was the twenty-second of December. In the East the battles had come to an end. Now the battalion was traveling west.

Traveling west . . . the word made the soldiers shudder. The war in the East — so said all the men who had come over from the West — that Russian-Polish war was child's play compared to what was happening on the western front. Surely that could not be true! Had they not suffered enough already? Was there to be no one left? "The West" had the ring of a death sentence.

It was a long time before they reached Ostrowo on the German frontier again. The train was always stopping at tiny stations, sometimes out in the fields, to be overtaken by other trains carrying cannon, machine guns, fodder, and provisions.

On a siding at one small station stood a baggage car loaded to the roof with parcels. Four soldiers, under the supervision of a corporal and a sergeant, were rummaging about among them. When Ru asked what they were doing, the sergeant said that their divisional commander had ordered the packages addressed to him and his staff to be found at once. They were now searching the second carriage for them.

"Who are those parcels for, the ones that have fallen out?"

"For the troops," said the sergeant, still burrowing into the pile. Another shower of soldiers' packages fell to the ground, regardless of all the care and love with which they had been packed by wives and sweethearts. There were homemade cakes in them, and brandy, tobacco, dried sausages and dripping — saved up over the months and now fallen among the rails while their intended recipients waited in slit trenches and dugouts for their Christmas presents.

"Oh, thou joyful, oh, thou blessed, gracious gift of Christmastide!" hummed Dambach as they clambered back into their cattle cars.

"Well, Ru," said Alert, when the lieutenant returned to his compartment. "Have you finished that war diary for today?"

"Yes, Captain."

"You'll be reading it out to your pupils one day, eh?"

"If the time comes, I will," said Ru.

"Then don't leave anything out, my dear Professor! May I see what you've written there? No secrets, are there?" said Alert with a grin.

"Of course!" said Ru, handing him the book. Alert began to read, but after only a few words he struck the armrest with one hand: "That's wrong, that's absolutely wrong," he said. "I'm sorry, my dear Ru, but every word is an untruth!"

Ru paled. He was not aware of having lied, he had seen the world, he was a teacher and an officer. Did he have to take this, even from a superior? "Would you be so kind, Captain, sir, as to show me one single lie in there?"

"Now, now, now, don't be so formal. We're talking man to man now, my dear Ru. I'll tell you what I mean," said the White Raven. "Look here, you've written: 'The Russian-Siberian troops defending Height 181 fought like lions. The hill looked like a common grave.' Now, I ask you, have you ever seen a lion fighting? Do you imagine that a lion runs a bit of pointed metal into its opponent's guts, turns it round, and pulls it out again? Does a lion throw hand grenades and blow a hundred other lions into a hundred thousand pieces? Have you ever heard of one of the higher beasts killing his like by the thousand? I can only tell you that a real lion would not thank you for the comparison. The lion is generous — everyone knows that. No generosity is permitted in the soldier. And then: 'Height 181 a common grave,' where were your ears, Professor? Does a grave utter shrieks of pain? Oh, no, before you tell your pupils about it, have another look, and when you soon stand, as I hope with all my heart you do, at your desk again, tell your class what it was really like, without those deceptive phrases they used to mask the truth from me when I was only a cadet. And then, don't forget our Panie!"

"By no means," said Ru, visibly moved by his superior officer's words. "That boy has kept his heart pure even in war. He really was sent to us by God."

"Do you know," said Alert, "I'd like to give him something, too, if only I could think what."

"Yes, of course, it's Christmastime," said Ru, "we must get some nice little surprise for him. How about a watch?"

"He can have that, too, of course," said the White Raven, "but I was actually thinking of something else, something more in line with what he's done, a kind of compensation for not getting an Iron Cross or promotion. Perhaps Allenstetten can think of something."

"Allenstetten!" Ru called to the next compartment.

The lieutenant appeared, and when the problem was put to him he suggested a horse.

"A horse?" Ru and Alert roared with laughter. "Panie high up on a horse, that's a marvelous way to hide him!"

"Perhaps I'll think of something more suitable," said Allenstetten rather crestfallen. "Give me time."

"Please, not an aquarium or a stamp collection!" choked Ru. "He won't have much use for a football on the western front, either."

"Absolutely not," said von Allenstetten. "I know what we'll do! We'll put in an application for Jan to be given German citizenship. Then he'll no longer be a Russian subject, we shan't have to hide him, and he can sit on his high horse. He'll be a German — perhaps he could be recommended for the Iron Cross at the same time."

"That's a splendid suggestion," said Alert. "You put the application in hand right away and I'll approve it as battalion commander and pass it on to the High Command."

In the last flat car, Dambach was relieved by Voss. Jan had also had enough of guarding the gun. After all, no one was going to come and steal it, and he was cold, too.

But it was warm in the horse cars. Flox had already spent the whole day in one of those, with drivers Müller, Uhl, and Podlesch. A big horse is like a stove. At the next stop, Jan climbed into the mobile stable, taking Cordes, who had been stamping around outside trying to warm his feet, in with him. Now there were five of them with the four horses on the straw in the middle of the wagon. A petroleum lamp smoked over their heads. The horses trampled the floor with their feet, and when the train swung round a bend they stumbled together. Jan took out his mouth organ and played a song none of the others knew, a melancholy air that he had learned from Vladimir the shepherd. The train wheels turned in time to its rhythm.

Suddenly Jan stopped, wiped the mouthpiece on his sleeve and put the instrument back in his pocket. "This can't go on much longer," he said, almost to himself.

"What do you mean?" asked the pockmarked Podlesch. "What's not going to go on?"

"It's just what I think," said Jan, falling silent again. But Podlesch would not let it drop and Müller joined in. "Go on, say it!"

"Don't know," said Jan. "It just came into my mind."

"What?"

"All that with me and Vladimir and my people, you know, Cordes, it can't go on like this." And from his pocket he took a crumpled card, smoothed it out and said: "My father wrote this, it was in the New Testament, beside Vladimir, you saw it lying in his blood, Cordes. The card was marking the bit about the Prodigal Son. . . ."

He hauled the thin book out of his trouser pocket, opened it, and read: "And he arose, and came to his father. But when he was yet a great way off, his father saw him, and had compassion, and ran, and fell on his neck, and kissed him. And the son said unto him, Father, I have sinned against Heaven and in thy sight, and am no more worthy to be called thy son."

There was complete silence in the car. Only the horses' hooves thumped dully on the floor. Cordes nodded his head and pointed to the card: "Can I have a look?"

"You won't understand it, it's in Polish," said Jan. "What does he write?"

And Jan read, first a few words in Polish, then the same thing in German: "Dear Vladimir, Please send the four rubles I lent you to Peter — That was my uncle," Jan interjected — ". . . dear Vladimir, if you have not got the four rubles, send me some ointment for my feet, they're finished, do you still have to walk everywhere? Peter never writes. Haven't you any news from Kopchovka? For the four rubles he must buy Jan a jacket, it's cold. Don't forget we're going by train now but nobody knows where. Your friend, Kubitzky. Dear Vladimir don't forget the four rubles. Peter must give Goloborotka twenty kopeks to write and tell me about Jan. Don't forget."

"So that's why you think it can't go on like this?" asked Cordes after a moment. Jan nodded and stroked Vladimir's dog, who was lying beside him, but his thoughts were far away: Don't forget . . . don't forget. . . . He thought of the telephone cable in the forest of Dombie that he had mended, of Alert's orders that had come down that wire, destroyed Dombie, and killed Vladimir. He did not fold his hands together but inside him the prayer went on: Father, I am no more worthy to be called thy son.

But nine cars farther up, in the staff section, von Allenstetten was sitting opposite Alert, reading out what he had written: ". . . It is therefore proposed that in consideration of his exceptional services on behalf of the German troops during the World War, Jan Kubitzky who is German in language and German in sensibility, should be granted German citizenship."

"I don't think they will refuse us this," said Alert, folding up the large white sheet on which the application was written.

"After all, it is something for our Propaganda Department, too," said Ru. "That kind of thing gets in the papers. Skillfully done, it's by far the best way of encouraging a warlike spirit in the country and pepping up sagging enthusiasm. Think of it: a German Joan of Arc!"

"So the result of that," said Alert, frowning, "would be that Jan was doing something for us yet again. That's not really the point of a gift."

"But the honor," said Allenstetten, "think what an honor it would be for the boy! With a war on, he might well become a warrant officer."

"I wonder if we're doing quite the right thing?" said Alert thoughtfully. "How is it that the youngster has achieved all these wonderful things, can you tell me that?"

"How? Well, because he's a bright boy."

"Hm, I suggest that quite a lot of our people are

that," said the White Raven, lighting a cigar. "I think it goes a bit deeper. I have the impression that he's been able to do it only because he is a completely free human being, actually the only free person of them all — the rest are just obeying orders. This boy is not relying on some superior officer or some regulation, he works entirely on instinct. As soon as he became a soldier I'm afraid his instincts would wither and his natural feelings would be blunted. He would just be jumping to it like all the others, on the principle that the soldier need not think. Oh, yes! Hold your tongue and sing 'Watch on the Rhine'! That's the way the whole system works."

Ru and Allenstetten glanced at one another. They obviously did not agree, but since the White Raven was their superior officer, they had to keep quiet.

Next morning the frontier was crossed again, but this time the men did not rejoice, because they knew where they were going. Their own country, through which they were traveling now, was simply a thin band, stretching from one German frontier to another, one narrow, iron band of rails. But where it ended, on the western front, death was waiting impatiently for them to arrive.

❖ JAN IS GRANTED A WISH

O N CHRISTMAS EVE THEY CROSSED THE ODER and before dawn they crossed the Elbe Bridge at Dresden. Jan was beaming. Wonderful, how the arches of the bridge soared from one bank to the other as if it were a mere trifle to carry all the heavy trains across the river! This was something quite different from the bridge across the Ravka at home, and yet that, too, was a good piece of work. But here — eighty meters in one span from pillar to pillar. How was it done? Extraordinary that iron can be so light, can fly! And those railway stations — Dresden-Neustadt, Dresden Central, each a paradise for the great steam engines.

And so that the poor soldiers should not feel completely excluded from that paradise, kind ladies poured coffee for them from great white jugs and they could help themselves to sandwiches, as many as they wanted, from big wooden trays. "You'll only find the likes of this in Saxony," said Rosenlöcher, who had been talking nonsense ever since they crossed the border. "Such bee-yootiful coffee, handsome stations, pretty girls!" When the train moved off again he perched with Mustard, Jan, and Flox in the doorway, eyes and legs hanging out and mouth working nineteen to the dozen, even when it was full. He was talking so as not to think. He was laughing so as not to cry. His chest was tight with homesickness. He saw his beloved country and yet could not set foot in it. His heart hurt him, beating fast and hard.

At the next station, followed by Jan and Flox, he ran up to the engine and asked the engineer if they would be traveling through his own part of the province. He did not even dare to think of his hometown, Plauen, which seemed like a distant dream. But the engineer knew nothing, he was only going as far as Chemnitz. They ran back to their car and in Chemnitz they ran forward yet again. Papa gave the new engineer a cigar, and when the man recited the names of the stations, and the name of Plauen was included, he gave the stoker his last five cigarettes. "Have we time to send a wire?" he asked excitedly. "Got to tell the wife, so she can come to the train, and Oskar, too." But there was no time. They ran back again.

"Hey, Rosenlöcher," called Jakob from his compartment, "what's all this running up and down? Have you gone mad?"

"Not mad, just Saxon," panted Papa.

"Then get in here, quick, and you too, Jan, or the train will leave under your noses!" When they were in the compartment with him, he asked, "Well, Jan, how do you like it in Germany? You haven't seen much, of course, only stations — "

"The stations are beautiful," said Jan, "the one in Dresden — "

"Oh, you ought to see Frankfurt station! If we go through Frankfurt . . ."

" 'Scuse me, Sergeant," Rosenlöcher interrupted. "You was a lawyer in peacetime, right?" Jakob assented. "Right then, Doctor (that right?), I want to ask you something about law. I've got this little company, Albin Rosenlöcher, Groceries and Agricultural Products, in Plauen. You send your bill to my firm, it'll be paid straight off."

"Stop talking rubbish, Rosenlöcher. What is it you want to know?"

"Look, here, Doctor: there's my business there in Plauen and here am I, sitting in this train. So I mean to say, there is Plauen, there is my business, and the train goes — "

"So you want to take a quick spot of leave?" asked Jakob, smiling.

"You're a clever lawyer, you catch on fast!"

"But it's not up to me to give you leave."

"I know, I know," said the grocer, "but being a lawyer, perhaps you can tell me the best way to get it. I wouldn't mind giving a whole case of cigars for it."

"Don't do anything foolish, Rosenlöcher. That's bribery. We don't have that in the army."

"Sergeant, far as I'm concerned, you're a lawyer just now. Have you ever seen a sergeant who didn't take a cigar where he could find one? That's a laugh! For a spot of leave, two days even, I'd pay a thousand marks and be happy."

"Then I'll tell you something, Mr. Rosenlöcher," said the lawyer. "If you really insist on bribery, you go and offer your money to the top brass — the highest of all. They'll take it."

"Who?" asked Rosenlöcher, staring flabbergasted at the lawyer. "You mean Alert?"

"Rubbish!" exclaimed Jakob. "The German Reich, the State."

"I think you're trying to make a monkey out of me," said Rosenlöcher. The train stopped at the next station and Jakob pointed through the window at a poster portraying the commander-in-chief, Hindenburg, over the caption: "Lend for the war effort!"

"War's bad business for the likes of us," said Rosenlöcher. "Anyone who puts his money into that won't see it again too soon. I want a bit of leave, that's all."

"Then you invest your money in that bad business," the lawyer advised. "Leave to make a war loan would be approved."

"I'd even give two thousand marks," said Rosenlöcher. "How about arranging things for me with the battery commander now?"

"No, no, you'd better do it yourself. I'm the sergeant again now."

Rosenlöcher scratched the back of his head. Von Allenstetten was no pushover. If only it had still been the White Raven, who had a kind heart and was always ready with a friendly word, but to go directly to him now would be against the rules.

The train stopped at a freight station. Papa plucked

up his courage, ran forward, and climbed onto the step of the officers' compartment.

"The officers are eating now," said one of the stewards. "I'm not allowed to disturb them. What do you want, soldier?"

"It's . . . um . . . it's about . . . it's a matter of national importance," stammered Rosenlöcher.

"Come back in an hour, then."

Albin Rosenlöcher trotted laboriously back again to his cattle car, where Jan was waiting. Papa had to lie down for a little, his heart was beating so furiously. "Just feel it!" he told Jan. Jan felt his heart through the uniform, beating and beating, more violently than the clatter of the car they were sitting in. Dambach unbuttoned Rosenlöcher's collar. "Get water!" he told Jan at the next stop. Papa looked at his watch: another forty minutes and the officers would have finished their meal.

Jan brought the water, and Dambach made compresses. Papa lay flat on his back with his eyes closed. The train moved and stopped and moved and stopped and moved.

"Next station Reichenbach," muttered Papa, "I must get out there." He sat up abruptly. He buttoned up his uniform, replaced his helmet, and buckled it. Jan helped him, because Papa was having trouble, and he helped him to climb down and go forward as well.

Rosenlöcher stopped by the officers' car: "He might say no . . ." He looked anxiously up at the windows. There stood von Allenstetten, his back to the window. Helplessly, irresolutely, Albin looked about. "Think I should ask the lawyer? . . ."

"Don't worry," said Jan, "I'll ask Allenstetten," and he jumped onto the running board.

"Tell him I'll give four thousand marks to the war loan. I'll sell our garden," Rosenlöcher called anxiously, but Jan was already inside the door.

"Ah, there's our Jan of Orleans, our Jan of Arc!" cried Ru, catching sight of him in the corridor through the windowpane of his compartment. "Come in here, Jan," he called. He had been playing skat with Doctor Jürgensen and Lieutenant Zimmermann of the Eighth Battery.

"Tell me, my boy," he began, "what would you really like? It's Christmas Eve today and in Germany the children will be writing out their wishes for Santa Claus. There must be plenty of things you want."

"Oh, yes," Jan said, "but can I have them?"

"Well, wish for something, wish away," said Zimmermann, laughing. "We'll tell you if it's too dear."

"I can't wait to know what's coming," said the doctor.

"Rosenlöcher is out there," said Jan, "but he doesn't dare come in. He comes from Plauen and that's going to be our next station."

"So?" said Jürgensen. Jan glanced out of the window. Papa was standing on the platform, gazing upward, and Jan could almost feel his sick heart pounding.

"Well, Lieutenant, sir, I wish that Rosenlöcher could get out in Plauen and go and see his wife and his little boy."

"No other wishes?"

"No, sir."

"Good lad!" said Ru. Then he went to the next compartment, where Alert and Allenstetten were sitting. Jan gave Papa an encouraging wave through the window. The whistle blew, Papa stepped onto the running board and clutched the door handle. The train moved off.

"According to divisional orders," said Allenstetten, when Ru had passed on the boy's message, "leave over Christmas is permissible only in an emergency. This regulation — "

"This regulation," the White Raven intervened, "is the sort that stifles all the soldier's enjoyment, all his goodwill. But I'll obey it to the letter. What did you say? Only in an emergency? This *is* an emergency. It would bring shame on the whole battalion to deny its savior a request, and one that springs from the soldier's noblest emotion: comradeship."

"I'll do the necessary at once, sir," said von Allenstetten. "Leave to the evening of the twenty-seventh," and he turned to the door.

"Stop!" shouted Alert: "Only on one condition: only if he takes the youngster in as a guest over Christmas."

"Very good," said Ru. "That will give little Panie a chance to learn how we Germans celebrate Christmas. Since he'll soon be a German himself — "

Papa was still standing on the running board of the moving train, both hands clamped to the door handle. He did not dare open the door — it might be contrary to regulations to get into the officers' carriage without permission, who could tell, and if it was and he did it, that would be an end to his leave.

But when Jan, beaming all over his face, let down the window and shouted "Leave!" Rosenlöcher almost fell off the running board for joy and weakness. Jan clutched his arm and pulled him through the quickly opened door. "You can keep your money, Papa, you won't have to sell your garden. But you've got to take me with you, or they won't do it. Will you take me with you?"

Then Papa gave the boy a kiss.

"Green, not in summertime alone, but even in the winter snow, O Tannenbaum, O Tannenbaum," Albin Rosenlöcher sang in a thin voice as they passed through the familiar villages of his homeland, and he began to bloom, to breathe, to revive, like a caught fish thrown back into the water. In the cattle car they were all standing around him, repeating over and over again: "Man, you're in luck! Aren't you lucky, man!"

"Panie going too?" asked Mustard.

"And Flox," cried Jan. Hearing his name, Flox jumped up at him in delight, having become aware when the kit bags were packed that they would soon be leaving the crowded, stifling car.

"Will you be coming back to us?" asked Mustard.

"What do you mean, Mustard? I'm your Panie, aren't I?"

"For sure?"

"For sure. Good-bye! Good-bye! Good-bye!"

Plauen! "Good-bye!"

"Leave is the best life insurance," said Dambach, watching Rosenlöcher as he hurried along the platform with Jan. Then he tipped the water he had used for the compresses out of the doorway.

❖ WE WISH YOU
A MERRY CHRISTMAS

TREES ALIGHT WITH CANDLES SHONE BEHIND the windows of the houses. The streets were empty, but here and there Christmas carols rang out through the night air. Jan wanted to stop and listen, but Albin urged him on. "Just a bit further down, and we're home." When they turned the third corner he positively shouted, "There! You can see it now, that light house down there, with the black sign on it." On the black sign was written in white letters: Albin Rosenlöcher, Groceries and Agricultural Products. It ran across the top of three shop windows. Albin puffed out his breath. He had actually gotten to see his shop again!

"Look there, that's our tree shining up there, too!" He pointed to the window above the sign.

But for all his impatience he mounted the steps very slowly, stopping several times to rest. Jan took his pack, and he straightened up again. "Never had such trouble with them steps before," he murmured. From above the words of a song floated down to them: ". . . in

David's town this day is born of David's line...."
Whose were those clear voices?

At last they were standing at the front door. "We're here," said Albin, his forehead now pearled with sweat. "Yes," he said, running his finger over the nameplate. "That's me: Albin Rosenlöcher, right. And now, watch!" He pressed the doorbell, Flox barked, a door inside was opened, quick footsteps came along the corridor — Rosenlöcher gripped Jan's arm hard — the door opened and the hall lamp shone in a pair of astonished eyes.

"Sissi!" cried Rosenlöcher. "That's wonderful," and he stretched out his arms to her.

"Uncle, oh, Uncle, what's that little dog you've got there?" Flox bounded around them, barking, and their laughter rang up the passage. A door was flung open behind the girl. "What's that dog — " cried a boy, scarcely older than Sissi.

"Oskar!" cried Rosenlöcher.

"It's our Papa!" cried Oskar, and his voice cracked — it was just breaking.

Kisses, more kisses, and hugs. Mrs. Rosenlöcher rubbed her cheek against her husband's unshaven one. "Now, how are you then, Selma?" "And you, Albin?" Behind them two old people, Papa's parents, were standing in the doorway, rumpled and blissful. "We just been talking about you, Albin," said the old man, and the old woman added: "Now, let him in. Come straight from Russia, have you? Let me look at you!" She drew him into the living room. "You don't look too good. Is anything the matter, Albin?"

"Jan! Where is Jan? Bring Jan in here!" In a moment Oskar had taken Jan's hand, while Flox gobbled down one of the biscuits hanging on the Christmas tree.

"That dog eats Christmas trees!" cried Sissi, shaking with laughter.

"Watch out he doesn't pull the tree over!" warned Mrs. Rosenlöcher.

"Is this the Jan you're always writing to us about, Papa?" asked Oskar, looking the other boy up and down.

"Of course, who else?" said Papa. "There's only one of him in the world. You thank him Oskar, he saved your Papa's life. Without those two" — he pointed to Flox and Jan — "your Papa would be at the bottom of the swamp. He got me my leave, too."

"Oh, come on, Rosenlöcher, don't tell stories!" said Jan, embarrassed.

"What's this Rosenlöcher all of a sudden? You can keep on calling me Papa. That young 'un may be my Oskar, but I'll always be your Papa. And here's Mamma and here are the grandparents." But Jan was more interested in Sissi.

"My niece Elizabeth," Albin remarked, "my brother Anton's daughter. He's in the service, too."

"In the West," said Sissi, her laughter suddenly wiped away. "Have you had a look at our tree yet, Mr. Jan?"

"Time for that later," said her aunt. "Soldiers are hungry, and we've got carp." While she and Sissi added two more places at the table, Father Albin was whispering with his son. Then Oskar took Sissi on one side

and there was a great deal of mysterious toing and fro-
ing. Meanwhile Rosenlöcher and Jan went to the bedroom and washed thoroughly, which was very
necessary after their long journey.

"It's all right with you, isn't it?" Mrs. Rosenlöcher
asked her husband when he came in again. "My asking
Sissi. Your sister-in-law has enough on her plate with
four!"

"You've asked Sissi, I've asked Jan," said Albin, putting his arm around her shoulders. "So we've both got a
war baby. Eat up, Jan, tuck in! But watch out, there's
plenty of bones in that carp!"

Sissi and Oskar glanced meaningly at each other and
before the meal was over they were doing something
behind the tree, among the glittering branches, fragrant
candles, and bobbing apples. Jan caught sight of
pink cheeks and sparkling eyes and heard the rustle of
paper and giggles. Then a little bell rang and: "Santa
Claus coming, Santa Claus coming for Jan!" declaimed
Oskar. Sissi took Jan's hand and pulled him toward the
tree. "This is yours," said Oskar. The children had
hastily gathered together everything a boy like Jan
could need. There was a rucksack that Oskar had used
only twice, Oskar's bicycling breeches that Papa had
bought him the spring before, socks, a pullover, and
two sports shirts. Grandfather had added a five-mark
piece: "To buy something for yourself!"

"Don't be cross, Auntie!" Sissi whispered to Mrs.
Rosenlöcher, for now was the moment for the special
gift: there, in its leather case, was a fine wristwatch,

from Sissi. Her aunt had given it to her for Christmas just an hour before.

That night Jan slept in a real bed for the first time in his life, a bed with soft feathers and white bed linen. Ahhhh! He had never slept like this before. He slept until the next afternoon, until Sissi's watch, which he had not taken off, showed a quarter to two. He washed quickly and put on his new clothes: a shirt, breeches, and a belt, long socks, and a pullover. This was better than a uniform! At the same time he admired Oskar's bicycle, which spent the winter in his bedroom. He spun the pedals, felt in the toolbox, and tried out the bell. At its ring Oskar, Sissi, and Flox, who had been waiting impatiently, appeared at once.

Mrs. Rosenlöcher's old bike was on the ground floor, and the boys pumped up the tires immediately after lunch. Then the two bicycles were wheeled out on the street. Oskar showed Jan how to mount, then hung onto the saddle, and gave orders: "Push down firmly, same both sides, don't hang on to the handlebars like that!" and ran alongside: "Same both sides!" Jan ped-aled so fiercely that the saddle slipped from his teacher's hand. "Watch out!" shouted Oskar and *bump*, Jan was lying on the tarmac.

"Beginning is always the difficult part," said Sissi, laughing as she picked up the bike. But after four more falls Jan could bicycle down the street on his own. Sissi pedaled alongside, ringing her bell and shouting with laughter, her curly mop fluttering in the wind. Now

they had turned the corner, hurrah! And then straight on, without even looking back.

Oskar was left standing dumbfounded in the road. "Faithless woman!" he moaned, after he had waited some time. "First sight of a uniform and I'm right out of the picture, wait and see!" He trotted glumly back to the house and through the back entrance into the shop, where he found his father and grandfather busy with books, barrels, boxes, and bins.

"There's nothing left in them, you've got nothing left," said Albin, shaking his head wonderingly. "Where're all the provisions gone?"

"Goods are short," said Grandfather, "everything's getting dearer and dearer. We don't get anything more in: think of all the stuff we used to get from abroad! Coffee, tea, rice, all the tropical fruits, spices, and petroleum, and oil, too. If they don't get this war over soon. . . ."

Sissi and Jan were far away. The town lay behind them, and they were on a steep hill where they had to push the bikes.

"My father is fighting, too," Sissi told him.

"Mine too," said Jan.

"My mother is so worried about him," Sissi went on, "is yours?"

"My mother's dead."

Sissi took her hand off the handlebar and stroked Jan's arm. "Oh, Jan, you poor thing. Was it long ago?"

"It's been a year now," said Jan, the tears coming

to his eyes. Sissi dropped her bike, took his face in her hands and kissed him. "Don't cry, Jan, don't cry!"

Later that afternoon the family went for a walk. What with learning to ride a bicycle and Sissi, Jan had seen nothing of the town, but now he looked about him with wide eyes. All the streets had the names of people, mostly poets and artists. And the shops were brightly lit — and the inns — they were quite different from Goloborotka's little tavern in Kopchovka! They turned in at a door, where pretty waitresses were running to and fro, a dozen to a room, serving coffee, beer, and cake.

"Hey, Mr. Rosenlöcher!" someone called. "Well, where did you spring from? I thought you were in Warsaw already!" It was Mr. Nockel, who had the barber's shop around the corner from the Rosenlöchers', a dry little man with a wart on the side of his nose. "Come and sit with us. Move over a bit, Clara! Spill the beans now, what have you been up to all this time?"

Rosenlöcher told him, but the little man just repeated drily: "Oh, come on, come on!" It was enough to drive anyone mad. When Albin told him how many men in the battery had lost their lives out there, the man shrugged his shoulders disparagingly: "Oh, come on, that's nothing! Do you have any idea what's going on in the West, in Flanders? Forty thousand dead in fourteen days. Bottoms up!" He gulped down some beer, wiped his mouth, and said, "Young fellows, all of them, straight out of school into the bright and breezy war. That was something, the way the boys stormed Langemarck!"

"Can I sock him one in the kisser?" asked Jan.

"Sshhh!" went Albin. Nockel was a good customer, he mustn't mess things up.

"Oh, yes," said Mrs. Nockel, who was as fat as her man was thin, "you should see how my husband gets worked up about the war, it's terrible! Reads all the papers; now he's got a map of all the war centers. Wherever our troops are, he sticks in a little black-white-and-red flag."

"Wonderful!" said Rosenlöcher, digging Jan in the ribs.

"Oh, yes, you should hear him," Mrs. Nockel went on, "you should hear the row my hubby makes whenever you retreat somewhere!"

"Oh, come on," said the barber, becoming quite lively. "Aren't I right? It shouldn't happen, it's sheer cowardice. Forward! Ever forward! That's what our crown prince said, and he should know, shouldn't he? You people in the East should have taken Warsaw long ago. You need to pull yourselves together!"

"You'll have to set us an example, Mr. Nockel," said Rosenlöcher, whose patience was giving out. "Why aren't you out there yourself?"

"Flat feet," said the little man, shaking his head. "Not a thing I can do about it, more's the pity. But if I were at the front — "

"Oh, if my hubby was at the front," his wife interrupted him, "he would have died a hero's death for our

beloved fatherland in the first attack. It's always the
same, they say: it's the best that fall."

"Then you must excuse me, Mrs. Nockel, for not
having cashed in my chips," retorted Rosenlöcher
grimly. "I'll take the very next opportunity to remedy
the oversight," and he stood up.

"Oh, come on!" said Nockel. "We were having such
a cozy chat. Must be nice for you uniformed men to be
back in the dear homeland for once."

But Rosenlöcher had had enough.

When they got back to the house and opened the
door, they saw something lying on the floor. A telegram. Albin opened it. Then he went swiftly to the
kitchen.

"What is it?" asked his wife anxiously. "You haven't
got to go back right away, surely?"

"No," said Albin, handing her the telegram.

"Your brother?" She read the telegram: ". . . fallen
. . . Oh, God, poor Elsie — and the children, poor
Sissi — "

"My parents — " groaned Albin. "My parents —
how are we to tell them?" They stood there, helpless
and despairing.

In the living room the children had lighted the candles on the tree. Now they were singing, and Jan was
accompanying them on his mouth organ: "We wish
you a Merry Christmas and a Happy New Year!" Rosenlöcher called his father, and Grandmother's eyes
widened with anxiety. What were they keeping from
her? She followed her husband out to the kitchen.

The telegram had fallen from the old man's shaking hands and she stooped and picked it up. "My Anton, my — " The tears poured down her cheeks while pitiful sobs shook her shoulders. "But you were still so young, Anton, you would have had so long to live!"

Tears, tears. "Does it have to be like this?" she screamed suddenly. "God, does it have to be?"

Jan was standing beside Sissi, by the tree on which the candles were still burning: "Oh, Sissi, you poor thing!" He tried to dry her tears, to comfort her, but fresh tears kept flowing down her cheeks, which had been bright with laughter a moment before. "Don't cry, Sissi, don't cry — "

"Albin, Albin!" groaned the old woman in the kitchen. "Don't you die on me, too, oh, don't die!" And she clung to the arm of the only son left to her.

❖ GOD WILL PUNISH YOU

NEXT MORNING SISSI RETURNED TO HER mother and her family. Jan and Oskar took her to the train while the parents and grandparents sat at home, silent and wretched. Many thousands of parents and grandparents were grieving as they did then, countless children and brothers and sisters weeping. And every day brought more of them.

On Sunday, the twenty-seventh of December, Albin's leave would be over. Twenty-four hours to go, then only twenty. A sleepless night began.

Now there were only twelve. Suddenly a mere four hours were left. Four more hours of home.

Three hours. Darkness was beginning to fall, and at six they would have to go to the station. "Mother, you stay home," said Albin. "I'll say good-bye to you here. It's too much of a strain for you." But his mother would not hear of it: "If I knew I could, my Albin, I would go off to the war in your place and they could shoot me dead."

"Me too," said the old man, "we've lived long enough, but you. . . ."

"Be good, Oskar," said Rosenlöcher on the way to the station. "Don't give your mother any trouble, work hard at school, learn your sums! You'll have to take over the business when I'm not there anymore. It may not be long now." Oskar squeezed his father's hand: "But Papa. . . ." They walked on in silence.

"When do you think you'll be getting leave again?" asked Mrs. Rosenlöcher when they were at the station, waiting for the grandparents who were following slowly behind.

"Don't you worry, Selma," her husband soothed her, "I know how it's done, now. We've got a lawyer in our battery, a real sly fox, and he told me: best thing is, buy war bonds. They always give you leave for that."

"Well, sign on right away, Albin, we've got something in the bank."

"We could sell the garden, too," said Rosenlöcher.

"Our lovely garden?" cried Oskar in a fright.

"Hold your tongue, Oskar," said his mother brusquely. "If it would mean keeping your father away from the shooting even for one hour, you'd give up that little bit of garden." Oskar fell silent, ashamed of himself, but in his mind's eye he saw the beautiful garden on the edge of town, the lilac bushes surrounding it, the beds of narcissus, primula, and anemones, the strawberry patch, the orchard with its apples and pears, and he whispered to Jan, "If I could find out who started this dirty, cursed war, I'd pulp him to a jelly. I'll find out, you wait!"

They went through the barrier with eight minutes to spare. "I'd be sorry myself, Selma," said Rosenlöcher thoughtfully, "if we had to give up the garden, but believe me, fourteen days out there make me even sorrier, so if you see a chance of selling that land — "

"You there!" rasped an ugly voice all of a sudden. "Yes, you there, soldier!" as Rosenlöcher looked around in astonishment. "Can't keep your eyes open, what! Never learned to salute, what, what!"

"Major, sir!" gasped Albin, who had not seen his superior officer at all. He straightened to attention, hands at his side, thumbs in line with trouser seams. Selma, Oskar, and his parents stood by, thunderstruck.

"Scandalous — and deliberate, of course. I'll have your name!" the officer bawled. "Which troop?"

"Seventh Battery, Seventeenth Foot," panted Rosenlöcher. To be treated like this, worse than a criminal, under the eyes of his own son, his parents, and his wife. He gritted his teeth in order not to howl with rage.

"Don't grind your teeth at me, you! I'll drum that out of you: you'll give a salute marching past, this minute, and no mistakes! Back to the barrier, march!" he ordered. The people on the platform formed a passage as the gunner darted a pitiful glance at his wife. He did not dare to look at his parents at all. He trotted back to the station barrier.

"Can't you go any faster?" the officer barked. Papa, burdened with the heavy kit bag on his back, tried to trot faster still. It was like running the gauntlet. Red and black spots danced before his eyes as the fresh order came: "Halt! About turn!" For a second Rosenlöcher stood motionless, his face twitching, his right hand to his heart. Then he fell to the platform like an axed tree.

There was a scream, a mother's scream, from the old woman whose younger son had died a hero's death five days before and whose eldest was now being abused before her very eyes. She screamed so shrilly that the conductor forgot to give the signal to depart. The passengers stood transfixed at the train windows, two orderlies came running out of the Red Cross station, and the little old woman who had spent her whole life in quiet living, stepped up to the officer. "Shame," she said, "shame! God will punish you, all of you!"

Then she took off her coat, rolled it up and put it under the head of her son, who lay blue-lipped and shivering. She unhooked his collar and his belt, and when the orderlies tried to lift him, she would not let them go until she had asked: "Where to?" And when they said: "To the first-aid station," she said, "No, to the hospital. And I'm going too." One orderly took his legs, the other his shoulders, and with his mother holding her son's head in her hands, they moved off, Jan carrying belt and kit bag.

The officer had disappeared. The stationmaster gave the signal for the train to leave, and it moved out of the station.

That night, in his lovely, soft bed, Jan could not sleep. The old woman's scream was ringing in his ears: "God will punish you — all of you!" Whom? All those who torture other human beings and murder them and drive them to war. Thou shalt not kill, that was God's commandment. Think of the commandments, the old man in Gradicz had warned them. Have I obeyed God's commandments, have I obeyed Abraham's warning? Have I been the cause of someone's death? Once again he thought of the telephone line through the forest, of the people by the charcoal fire, of the dead bodies in Dombie, in Lutomirsk, in Kasimirsk. But he had only wanted to help his friends, to prevent anything happening to them! His friends? Had Vladimir not been his friend? Were Vladimir's friends any worse than his own? Perhaps they were having an even harder time than the men of the Seventh Battery, perhaps his father was having a worse time, too. Would he ever see him again? Would he ever see Cordes again, or Mustard? Alert? Ru? What might be happening to them while he lay here in Plauen in this warm, white bed? And Sissi, who no longer had a father? Sissi. . . .

He was filled with a great unrest. He tried to sleep, but he could not. There was something inside him that raged and stabbed, as on the day when he had mended the telephone wire and it had urged him forward to the observation post.

Suddenly he was out of bed, getting dressed, but not in uniform. He put that into his kit bag and put on his sports clothes. Then he picked up the paper in which the shirts had been wrapped and wrote on it: "Jan thanks you and hopes Papa will be well soon." He left it on the table.

Then he put Flox's collar on him and they quietly left the flat and walked back along the empty streets to the station he had left only a few hours before.

There was the platform on which Papa had lain. It was empty now, no train, no travelers. Sissi's watch showed twenty past one. What was he doing here? Why had he come here in the middle of the night? I could get myself a platform ticket the way Oskar did yesterday, he thought, I've got a bit of money.

He stood by an iron post at the barrier like a forgotten parcel, waiting, freezing, and alone.

At the last platform, where they had arrived on Christmas Eve, a train rolled into the station and stopped. Jan ran through the subway to see where it was going. It was a military train, endlessly long.

Scarcely had he reached it when everything came to life. Soldiers climbed out, fetched water, asked questions: "What time is it?" And: "What's this place called?" Jan answered and questioned them in turn: "Are you Pioneers?" And when they assented: "Were you on the Vistula, too?"

"Yes. What do you mean, too? Who else was there, youngster?"

"I was," said Jan. "Haven't you got someone with a red, pointed beard, an engineer?"

"Would his name be Papke?"

"Could be, I don't know his name. Where is he?"

The Pioneer started shouting: "Sergeant Papke! Papke! Papke!" The name traveled all the way down the train "Sergeant Paaaapke — Paaaapke — a visitor, a visitor for Sergeant Paaaapke!"

And sure enough, there he was, red beard and all, sleepy-eyed and not at all pleased at being disturbed, as he thought it was all a hoax. But when Flox jumped up at his old acquaintance, wagging his tail, and he saw Jan walking along behind him, he changed at once: "Where have you sprung from, my young colleague? How did you get hold of those fine togs?"

"Do you know where the Seventh Battery is?" asked Jan.

"It's gone to the western front, the whole division has gone. We're going there, too."

"Can I come?" asked Jan.

"In those togs? No question of it. You can't travel on military transport looking like that. Where have you left your uniform?" Jan laughed and pointed to his kit bag. "Get in then, you rascal! You can change inside."

And Jan climbed onto the train.

❖ PILLARS, PLATFORMS, AND PLANES

NOW JAN WAS WITH THE PIONEERS, TRAVELING through the Thuringian mountains, through valleys and forests, until they reached the Rhineland mountain range.

On the second day he saw the splendid bridges, carried by mighty pillars across the Rhine into the fine old city of Cologne. They were heading straight for Cologne Cathedral and as they stood at the window looking at the broad river through the iron trelliswork, Papke said, "Many bridges have been built across the Rhine, since a clever Roman called Julius Caesar built the first on wooden posts two thousand years ago. Bridges become stronger and more beautiful, but people — the Germans here and the French over in the West — have still failed to understand the purpose of the bridges. Can you imagine what these bridges want, my young colleague?"

"I believe," said Jan, "that they want people to be friends, as we are."

"If only they would!" said the engineer. "But instead

they misuse the good bridges for taking guns across, new ones all the time, and new cannon fodder, too."

Jan did not know which to admire most, these muscular bridges or the great, bright stations through which they traveled. Many trains stopped at Cologne, as they did; others were passing through, and everywhere the crowds thronged. Trolleys loaded with suitcases, papers, and drinks were pushed through the teeming mass. And then, suddenly, a distant droning: *zoommmm — zoommmm* and again: *zoommmm.* "Airplanes!" they all shouted. "Enemy airplanes coming!" The cathedral bells began to ring, and everybody hurried down the steps into the subways. In a moment the mighty station and all its platforms seemed to have been swept clean.

Down in the subway there was an excited, anxious buzz of voices: "If they drop bombs on the station we're done for! — No, they're going to attack the bridge!" That strong, young bridge, thought Jan. He felt as hurt as if it had been a living being.

But soon the news came through that the airplanes were heading southeast toward Koblenz. "Is there a bridge there, too?" Jan turned to ask the engineer, but he had disappeared, lost in the crowd.

Jan searched and with his sharp eyes he soon found him. In the general confusion, Eugen Papke had bumped into a school friend. His name was Heinz Wolfart, and he was going to the western front as an aerial observer, joining the troop transport at this point.

They traveled on to the front in fine, clean carriages, but their conversation went back to the days when they had sat side by side on the school bench, though it seemed to have happened only yesterday. The present, with its blood and tears, had vanished as they laughed till they cried over the remembered sayings of their old natural history teacher who had been wearing the same peculiar grey straw hat since the beginning of time. Wolfart imitated the singing teacher, purring through his gigantic beard, "In the woods the birds are sleeping, dawn is waiting — " bellowing, " — I'll box your ears if you fire any more paper darts!"

There was no end to the stories and jokes, a whole store of enjoyment that they had preserved from happier days and into which, now that joy had become a rare commodity, they plunged as into a grab bag. And the bag never emptied, for after school came dancing lessons and then the football club, engineering school, the holidays. They went off singing on mountain walking tours and climbed the steepest trail to every attainable peak.

Suddenly came the call to get out, they had arrived. Well, all right, thought Jan, but where? "Is this the West?" he asked the engineer.

"I'd like to know what the kid imagined the West really is," joked Wolfart. "Did you think it was a pub or something?" The West, it seemed, was as big as Poland, once blooming, well-established and fruitful, now a wilderness. Somewhere in this wilderness was the Seventh Battery, but where? How was Jan to find them?

"It doesn't really matter," said Papke, "you just stay with us, my young colleague. The word will soon go round that you're here, you and Flox, and then your battery commander will send word."

So Jan went on with the Pioneers, who were going to make an airport in a huge field and build hangars for the aircraft. It was astonishing to see everything springing up from the ground. Jan's eyes were everywhere, learning all the time. Now he was squatting in the workshop, now standing beside a drawing board, listening to explanations of the plans, but most of all he liked to watch the building going on, the iron stanchions joining, rising, and holding. This was his field, it even had things growing in it, and birds flying overhead: slender, shining aircraft. How he would have loved to fly with them, but whenever he asked Wolfart, the pilot would not hear of it. Jan watched longingly as the aircraft rose, circled the runway, and disappeared like a speck in the blue distance.

Was he really in the West now, the place of which his friends and Sissi and the family in Plauen had recounted such terrible things? But this was a paradise, not nearly as cold as his native land, and all around was peace. Peace?

Sometimes a dull grumbling and rumbling, lasting for days and nights, sounded from the distance, like a warning: don't count on peace!

Don't count on peace! Even those aircraft were not made for pleasure, not to raise people above the horrors here below. They were designed to make the misery on earth still worse, as Jan found out when one morning Wolfart explained the various types of aircraft to him: "These are observation planes — I'm flying in this one here today." Observation, thought Jan. That was just what he and Alert had been engaged in when they had climbed a hill or a tree together: searching for a target for the grenades and shrapnel.

"And back there are the bombers," Wolfart continued. Bombers? Bombing what? The bridges on the Rhine, which were supposed to make bonds between the nations? Railway stations, trains carrying people? Bombs dealing destruction on hangars like the ones they themselves had erected with loving care over the last week or two?

In the midst of his thoughts, he heard Wolfart's shout of laughter, felt himself grasped around the waist and lifted into the air, and in a moment he was sitting in an airplane. He thought he must be dreaming.

"Lieutenant Gutzeit gave permission," said Wolfart, "but make yourself as thin as you can so that no one from the control tower stops you. Here's Gutzeit coming now."

"Gutzeit!" Jan repeated delightedly. The week before Gutzeit had performed aerial acrobatics over the runway. "Where are we going?" He was glowing with excitement.

"Across the French front. We have to observe," said Wolfart.

"But what, who?" asked Jan eagerly.

"The wicked enemy, who else? I'm going to shoot up the Seventeenth Foot."

"Wha-at did you say?" Jan's mouth fell open. "Seventeenth Foot, Alert's battalion?"

"I wangled it pretty well, didn't I?" said Heinz Wolfart, as happy as a child. "What do you say now? This evening your Seventh Battery is going to take Hill 23 under fire. With the best will in the world they can't see anything from below, so it's up to us."

"But those are my people!" cried Jan, still beside himself.

"I know. So you can keep a sharp eye on them and see if they shoot well. Off we go!" The propeller was turned by the mechanic, the engine sprang to life. A rattling and thumping went through the aircraft, the wheels jounced over the stubble field and now, now they were hovering, now they were flying, flying like the swallows, as he had sometimes flown in dreams. . . .

But now it was real: there was Gutzeit at the controls and beside him sat Wolfart with a map in his hand and there below them was the roof of Hangar 1, the iron skeleton of Hangar 2, there the workshops, and the canteen! And it all looked so clean, as friendly as a set of toys, the fields brown as a deer's hide, fit to be stroked.

Is this what the earth looks like to God? thought Jan. But what were those broad stripes in the distance? Like ugly weals they cut straight across the country from right and left as far as the eye could see. The aircraft was flying straight toward them. Was this the front? The German and French positions, carved as if with crude knives into the very face of God's creation? Now he could see them clearly: slit trenches, communication trenches, support trenches, a whole network of them, and over that another net had been thrown, a net of barbed wire attached to posts hammered into the earth, on which the soldiers were caught as they made their assault and hung like targets for the bullets, fodder for the cannon. Did God see that, too?

Or was God looking down on earth from such a height that everything appeared to him simply as a stupid, childish game? That was how it looked to Jan himself, for without his noticing the plane had flown higher and was still rising. Forests became dark patches, a broad river was nothing but a thin, silvery thread. Infantry battalions looked like swarms of tiny midges, smaller than ants.

What drove these poor insects on to destroy themselves? They should have a good shaking, thought Jan, to bring them to their senses. He would like to spit on their heads.

Now they were vertically above the front, but there was no firing to be heard. The engine and propellers were making too much noise. Wolfart pointed to a place on the map, Hill 23, and then pointed down at something brown and humped in the pockmarked terrain and nodded. So that was Hill 23, looking no more than a molehill from above. Wolfart flashed a signal below. Jan peered down, narrowing his eyes. Now, to the left of the molehill, a small black dot like a spot of ink appeared. Another signal flash from above, another inkspot below to the right. Those must be shells, shells from his own battery. Like Lutomirsk five weeks ago, thought Jan. That had been a hill, too, Hill 181, and the Russians had dug their way into that hill, just as the French were doing here. And what looked like tiny ink splashes from above were shells landing.

Now the ink splashes were falling right on the molehill. The Seventeenth Foot had aimed well. Wolfart gave a last signal, and at that moment there rose before them, quite close to the nose of the plane, a grey cloud, then another, then a third, and a fourth: shrapnel clouds. Jan knew them only from below. Here they appeared to him in their true form: terrifyingly large, frighteningly near. The plane sideslipped to the right. It had been spotted from below and now the French antiaircraft guns were chasing it: another four shrapnel clouds. Something exploded a few feet below the wings. The aircraft spiraled steeply upward out of reach of the shrapnel clouds, but they still followed. The shells were exploding higher and higher, and if the plane were to be hit now it would go up in flames. There would be nothing to save them. But instead of falling they were still rising, steeply, rising at furious speed into the cloudless air above. The suddenly rarefied air hurt their ears.

Where were they? The floating clouds of shrapnel hid their view of the earth. Jan looked about him. According to the sun's position they must — but what was that? Over there, at the same height as themselves, *five specks*. Jan rose from his seat, tapped the pilot's shoulder, and pointed. Gutzeit looked quickly in the same direction and saw the dark specks against the bright sky. One was a little ahead, two on either side diagonally behind it. An enemy air squadron making straight for the reconnaissance plane.

In the same second Gutzeit grasped the joystick, and the airplane banked steeply to the right. But their pursuers must have had damned good machines. Gutzeit banked again and then raced straight back like an arrow across the two fronts.

The engine noise stopped, the thunder of the firing began. Soundlessly they slid downward in empty space. Jan's breath was snatched away, and he closed his eyes in the uncanny stillness. But suddenly the engine started up again and the plane began to climb higher and higher. The five enemy planes were very close now. Zzzzzz — came an almost constant whistling about Jan's ears. They had machine guns! If they should hit the engine, even with a single bullet, all three of them were lost. The engine stopped again, and once again the plane fell as if down an empty shaft. Jan's fingernails dug into his palms, trying to dull his wild excitement through pain. The chase lasted only a few minutes, but those few minutes encompassed the late of three people.

Where was the earth? Was it still there? There, it was coming nearer, quite near, very near.

Now they felt the ground under their wheels as they tore along the runway.

They were safe.

"My nineteenth reconnaissance flight," Gutzeit told Jan, turning toward the hangar. "If you hadn't been there, I would never have had a twentieth. Thanks very much, Jan. If we had seen them half a minute later they would have got us, those Englishmen! Hell, what a bit of work that was!" And he flung himself full length on the hangar floor.

Jan dropped beside him and so did Heinz Wolfart, all

three so exhausted that they could no longer stand.

When he opened his eyes, Jan saw Flox standing beside him, watching him with his intelligent eyes and wagging his tail. Then Jan got up. "Poodle, it's no good, we'll have to get back to the gun beasts. They're waiting for us."

"You're crazy," said Papke, when Jan took leave of him. "You'd have a hell of a good life with us. This is an oasis in the desert. Why won't you stay?"

"I promised," said Jan.

After a meal he packed his kit bag and set off: straight on, then right through a village, then left across a wide meadow, then right again, just as Wolfart had shown him on the map.

❖ THE BLACK STORM

A T LAST, THESE MUST BE THE GUNS OF THE Seventh Battery, here in this deep defile. Jan recognized them in the darkness, but it had been very difficult to find them. On a map that kind of thing looks easy. A hole had been dug deep into the side of the defile for each of the four cannon, but there was no sign of his friends. Jan called, and the guard came slouching up from the other end of the defile. This was an unknown face, a man with a crooked nose and some front teeth missing. "Where are the others?" asked Jan.

"First you tell me what you're up to here. Who are you anyway?" the guard exclaimed.

"Don't eat me up!" said Jan, giving his name: "Jan Kubitzky, known as Panie, Seventh Battery, Seventeenth Foot."

He had scarcely spoken when the guard began to grin all over his face: "Why didn't you say so straight off? So it's you, is it? You've been up to some pretty tricks, you scamp: Panie, I know! Mustard spends the whole day jabbering on about his Panie and Flox.

That's him, too, is it? Oh, yes, good doggie. Does he bite?"

"But who are you?" asked Jan impatiently.

"Me? Why, I'm Ziermann," said the guard. "Hannes Ziermann, if you must know: a lathe-operator by trade."

Now Ziermann in English would mean something like "dainty man" but this Ziermann was far from dainty — he even had one earlobe missing. "Nothing goes wrong when you're around, so I've heard," he chatted on. "They say you are a good angel, like. Hottenrot, that blabbermouth, was saying only this morn — "

"But where is Hottenrot? And Mustard? And the others?" Jan interrupted.

"Where would they be? Down there!" said Ziermann. "In the dugout," and he pointed to a trench to the right of the fourth cannon. About twenty steps had been cut into the side of the trench, leading downward. Jan clambered down. He was met by a gust of stifling air, but that didn't matter. There were his friends, lying or sitting on wooden benches. An oil lamp that had been with them when they were fighting in the East hung from the low ceiling, which was supported by wooden props.

The first to spot Jan was fat Dambach, now as thin as Rosenlöcher had once prophesied. "Attention!" he shouted. "His Excellency General Panie!" Then they were all on their feet: "Our Panie, our Panie!" His hands were seized, they were banging him on the back, and Flox was being fed with sausage skins. Cordes took

Jan by the shoulders: "Is it really you, boy?" His solemn face lit up.

"Make yourself comfortable, Panie," said Mustard, pushing his gear to one side. "This is our salon. What have you done with Rosenlöcher?" Jan put down his kit bag and told them what had happened at Plauen station.

"I'd have thumped that swine one," said Cordes grimly, "till his teeth came marching out of his snout in squadron formation. Nothing to lose. I could only have got prison and prison is better than the western front."

"He was in luck there, that Rosenlöcher," decided Hottenrot. "Better a heart attack than a direct hit. I'll write and tell him so. Perhaps he could send us something from his shop: coffee, sausage — has he got tobacco?"

Now some men arrived from other dugouts, first from the first and second gun crews to whom Ziermann had passed on the news, then from the supply wagons. For every one of the many new faces, one of the old familiar faces was missing, its owner wounded or dead.

But there, up the steps, came a familiar sight: a big, black, full beard and two faithful eyes: "Distelmann! Father Distelmann!" Jan shouted, running up the steps. "How's your hand getting on?"

"There, you can shake it again now. It could have taken a longer rest, but this war lasts for ever. It's long enough for the dead to be cured. I'm with the eighth wagon now and I'm to give you a kiss from little Freda. She's a big girl now!"

Jan had to tell his story again and they all had questions for him, but to the most urgent question — when there would be peace — Jan had no answer. When they heard that on that very morning he had been up above them in a reconnaissance plane and had nearly been shot down, they were tremendously proud: "Only our Panie could come through something like that!" said Dambach. One or two of the new men had actually seen the plane, and they, too, began to respect friend Panie: "I'll be damned, you have been up to your tricks!"

They brought out fried corned beef and chips. The corned beef had been taken from the English trenches. Cordes made coffee and distributed all the cigarettes from the packets he had received the day before: "It's a holiday today. We've got to live and let live. There, my boy, smoke!" But Jan did not take the cigarette. Cordes' dark eyes looked at him. "Dombie?" he asked quietly. Jan nodded.

Now everyone was talking, but there was not a lot to be learned. "Do you have to spend your time squatting down here?" asked Jan.

"Where else, man? Except when we have to stand to the guns!" Now they were all talking at once: "Man, you have no idea, oh man! You turn into a mole down here, we've got rats, too, Flox, you can chase rats, but partridge taste better, eh? Those brutes attack people, they nibble them, alive or dead, there's not much difference, after all. You've just no idea, my son. Have you heard who our oppo's are, over there with the *poilus*, the French troops? Africans, that's what, black as boot polish, I can tell you — "

By now Cordes had buckled on his belt and picked up his rifle. "Be seeing you, Panie, I must go on observation." Jan wanted to go, too. "No, my dear boy, you stay here. It's not for children and young dogs. It's a different wind blowing here in the West."

But Jan would not give in. "I must go and say hello to Alert. Flox can stay here."

It was about two o'clock in the morning. A great silence lay over the land as the two of them pressed forward through the long, muddy approach trenches. Here and there a rocket went up, creating a moment's daylight, but the trench was so deep that they could not see the rockets.

Then they reached the end. They had to cross the field for a stretch and that so-called field was a mass of shell holes, one after another, large and small. As each signal rocket went up, they had to throw themselves flat on their faces or duck into a shell hole to avoid having bullets whistling round their ears. Jan was dog tired, stumbling and slipping from one hole to the next. If he had had any notion of this abysmal place he would not have come. The flight that morning was still in his bones as well. It was too much for one day and for a boy not yet fifteen years old. For a moment he was afraid he was going to cry. Then he remembered Sissi. He remembered her often: her fresh face, which had laughed so unrestrainedly and wept so heartrendingly.

Don't cry, Sissi, don't cry, Jan!

They were there at last. The observation post lay behind a pile of earth at the corner of a wood, but there was nothing left of the wood. Ragged stumps and split branches stood like phantoms against the night sky. As a feeble protection against bullets and shell splinters, a layer of planks and earth had been laid over the observation post, but there was neither telescope nor observer there. Fifteen steps led down to the dugout. There they were.

Alert's eyes were moist when he saw the boy, but all he said was: "Well, then, you deserter, you!" Then he shared a bar of chocolate with him.

Ru was there, too. He had a curious, absent look, as if his nerve had gone completely.

"Why is no one observing?" asked Jan.

"There's nothing to observe at the moment," said Alert, pleased at the boy's interest. "The plane saw to that this morning. I can tell you, my boy, it was really terrific. Imagine, right up above us, about two or three thousand meters up, the pilot spots Hill 23, which we were firing on. We can't see it, can't see it at all, because there are hills in front of it and a railway embankment. We shoot at random according to the map, toward the general area, I look up through the telescope and see his signals: *short*, of course that means we're aiming short! We shoot a hundred meters longer and he signals: *long*, so that means too far. We shorten our aim by fifty meters again and there goes his signal: *long long short*. So, I calculate we should shorten the trajectory by another twenty-five meters. Two signals: *short long*, in other words, we've got it!"

"The last shot was only a tiny bit too far to the right," said Jan.

Alert looked dumbfounded: "Look here, how did you know that, Panie?"

"I was in the plane," said Jan.

"What a rogue," said Alert to Ru, who was staring indifferently straight ahead, "lets me tell the whole damned story and knows far more about it than I do all the time. Did we really hit the place?"

"Yes, sir."

"Distance correct, too?"

"Yes."

"This is very, very important. There may be an attack at any moment, from the very spot we're talking about. But now you must tell me what — " Howling, droning, and crashing snatched the words from his lips as thunder spewed from a hundred, many hundreds of cannon's mouths with a hammering as fearful as if iron fists were beating in their skulls. It seemed as if the whole world was being smashed to ruins, wiped out by machines gone mad. "Ghastly, ghastly, this is ghastly," stammered Ru, "those poor infantrymen!" No one else spoke. The thunder grew still more fearful outside. "This is madness!" cried Ru. "This is murder, murder, this isn't war anymore, this is — "

"Peace, is it?" Alert shouted savagely. "What was it you had in mind, Professor? Oh, yes, this is war. War is murder, Professor. Do you know how the French murder factory works? Two million employees, full-scale operations, branches halfway round the world. . . ." Then his voice could no longer be heard as the factory hammered on, the machinery thumping over their heads.

This went on for an hour, and for every one of its sixty minutes the factory delivered 110, 160, 190 dead men, 400, 800, 1200 casualties. Every one of them had once lain in his mother's lap, played between his father's feet, every one of them had learned to read, gone to school, sung songs, had friends, worked, loved, hoped. . . .

The observers sat in their dugout: Alert, Ru, Jan, Cordes, Signaler Strauss, Signaler Friedrich, staring at each other out of bleary eyes.

Suddenly there was silence outside, a deathly silence, but in the very same moment Alert shot up the stairs from the dugout with the others behind him, carrying the telescope. Now they stood crowded together in the observation post, the left-hand corner of which had been destroyed by a direct hit. Day dawned, grey on grey.

The telescope had scarcely been mounted when the pounding set up again, this time from the German department of the death factory. Now the German guns were doing precisely what the French had been doing for the previous hour. In a few minutes they, too, delivered many thousands of corpses, many thousands of cripples, all blacks.

They, too, had red blood, they, too, had once been held in their mothers' arms. Under the hot sun of their homeland they had grown big and strong, living a carefree life, enjoying the good fruits of their country, manioc, bananas, and pomegranates, delighting in music and dancing. Many of them were Christians. What were they doing here, in this strange, cold corner of the earth? What were they doing in this murder factory?

As if driven on by invisible whips, they rushed forward, countless long, solid lines of them, eyes and mouths opened wide: giants squeezed into uniforms, on they rushed, trampling the earth and yelling as if to drown the thunder of the cannon —

Tactactactactac tactactactactac the German machine guns rattled into the howling black storm, but although hundreds of black bodies fell to the ground, the others paid no heed. Wave after wave of them roared and raged forward over the fallen and as if to swell the uproar, they reached for the hand grenades on their belts and hurled them forty or fifty meters ahead: *crack! crack! crack!!!* "They're breaking through!" yelled Alert, glancing to one side. A German machine-gun post had been set up close to them, in a shell hole. Now it was turning its barrels on the black men who had already overrun the obstacle of the German front trench.

Closer and closer, higher and higher, the wild, grim wave rose toward them. Jan could already see the whites of the eyes in those black faces. Fear rose into his throat. *Tactactactactac* the new machine gun burst out to the left of him and in front of him the giants in their fluttering, khaki capes sank like grass to the sickle. Only one, a huge man, his cape flying, unfamiliar badges on his collar and sleeves, rushed on straight toward them, swung his arm with all his strength, flung the hand grenade — and fell. Was the missile for them or for the machine gun? Jan had no more time to think about it. A violent blow ... then darkness. He felt something warm trickling down his arm, and the world vanished.

He did not wake up until late that afternoon, to find himself lying in a bed, his arm heavy and painful.

When he opened his eyes, Cordes, pale and with a bandaged forehead, was sitting on the edge of his bed. "Hello, Jan, here we are again," he said, with a happy smile. "It worked out all right this time, too, Panie!"

❖ THE SKULL OF
SULTAN MKWAWA

J
AN AND CORDES HAD NOW SPENT FOUR DAYS IN
German Field Hospital XXXIV A, which had been
set up in the French boys' school at Neuville. What
was the point of boys' schools now? What was the
point of teaching and learning when even seventeen-
year-olds were being pushed into uniform and into the
death factory? The school benches and the big tables
from the classrooms could readily be chopped up for
firewood and fed into the stove. They were only in the
way in the classrooms, which were now filled with
crowded rows of iron bedsteads. To each was attached
a small board stating name and country of origin, if the
occupant was a prisoner, or for the German troops,
name, rank, and company. Jan's board said: Jan Kubitzky, volunteer, Seventh Battery, Seventeenth Foot.

"Volunteer? That's new!" said Jan, when he read it.

"Keep quiet. What else could I have said?" whispered Cordes. "That you're a Russian? And get you
pushed off into the prisoner-of-war camp when you're
better? That wouldn't suit Alert, nor Allenstetten.

They want to make a German of you. Haven't you heard anything about it?"

"No," said Jan in amazement. "Can that be done?" And he lay back on his pillows. He still felt rather weak.

"Of course," said Cordes. "After all, you're a Pole, not a Russian anyway, and whether you're a Russian Pole or a German Pole doesn't make a blind bit of difference, does it?"

That was too much for Jan's tired head. He closed his eyes and dropped off again.

The classroom where they lay was a blue-washed, airy room on the ground floor. Outside, in the school yard, mulberry bushes were growing, and when the windows were open you could hear the blackbirds singing.

Cordes was in charge. There were seventeen beds in the room, each with a wounded man in it. Apart from Jan, Cordes, and Voss, they were all prisoners. Cordes's and Jan's beds stood by the two pillars between the three big windows. Gunner Voss of the Seventh Battery lay on Cordes's left, diagonally under the window. It was very pleasant, close to the sky, the song of birds, and the fresh air.

In the five beds along the opposite wall lay five black soldiers. The songs they sometimes struck up in the evening sounded strangely exciting: sometimes a solemn plaint, sometimes a violent shaking, as if they were trying to cast off invisible chains. One had pulled the seat of a chopped-up school bench out of the wood supply heaped beside the stove. From it he carved figures that looked like goblins, with big heads, hats shaped like towers, and protruding eyes. Jan was given one of these figures, but the black man wanted to sell the rest and was helped in his trade by his neighbor, who answered to the name Ma-Ka. Ma-Ka spoke French, having played the violin with an orchestra in Paris for some years. It was a pity they had none here.

The black prisoners' beds were along the wall to the left of the door. Along the door wall, in the left-hand corner, lay four Frenchmen, three of whom groaned and whimpered ceaselessly in their fever. They had severe internal injuries and were not allowed to eat or drink. One of them, a farmer from Brittany, died that morning in terrible agony. He had been taken away now, and the bed was freshly made up. There was little hope for two others from the same area. When the chief medical officer, Dr. Willi Bohnsack, made his daily inspections he became graver and graver; and when he shook his head they knew the worst.

The fourth Frenchman was a handsome, powerful man, with dark, merry eyes, jet-black hair, and a little moustache. He had only a superficial neck wound, a great piece of luck, since the shot that had grazed him could easily have severed one of the great neck arteries. He often spoke of his vineyard at home in Ventron on the Alsatian border. The vineyard was his greatest worry, and it was difficult to tell which he feared more, vine lice or the army. If they should attack his grapes — oh, *mon Dieu!* He spoke German quite well, because it was only a stone's throw from Ventron, his own village, to Great Ventron, and Great Ventron was in Germany. He was a good-hearted man, who swept the room every morning and fetched and carried for everybody. He was keen on Nurse Veronica, a young girl with ash-blonde hair, whom he said he wanted to marry after the war. He had made friends with Jan on the second day and now they were inseparable. Because the Alsatian's name was Paul, Paul Fleury, the pair was nicknamed Jean-Paul. Voss, who was a bookbinder in Leipzig, had invented the name.

To the right of the entrance lay two British soldiers: Tommy Smith and Tommy Thomson. All the British soldiers were called Tommy. They called the French soldiers *poilu* and the Germans *Landser*. Tommy Thomson and Tommy Smith always had their teeth clenched on their pipes and talked a jibberish that no one understood.

"They're chewing the sole of an old shoe," Voss decided, and did that make Smith furious! He happened to have understood exactly what Voss said — in fact his German was very good, owing to a coincidence. His grandfather Schmidt had emigrated from Berlin to England in 1848 and translated his German surname into English. Now his grandson was with the Germans again and recited a German poem from memory, one he had learned from his grandmother as a child. When the nurse came to his bed to renew his dressings, he repeated it to her: *"Ich ging im Walde so für mich hin"* (I went for a walk in the woods alone). Nurse Veronica turned her head away. Poor Tommy, she thought, you will never go for a walk in the woods alone again. Tommy Smith had received a bad hip wound and his leg would probably be amputated next morning, though he knew nothing about it.

His friend, Tommy Thomson, had been much less unfortunate. Without touching his tongue and teeth, a bullet had passed straight through both cheeks. "How did you manage that?" asked Nurse Veronica, when she brought him his aspirins. "Were you shouting when the bullet hit you?"

"No, yawning," said Tommy Thomson. Tommy Thomson was a Scot.

Beside his bed hung the uniform of the Scottish troops, and as he was allowed to get up for the first time today, he put it on. Then even the very sick *poilus* had to smile, seeing the rangy blond giant in his short, colorful kilt, long stockings, and bare knees above them. "We need a getup like that for the Prussians!" chortled Voss, and Cordes called to Jan, "Imagine Dambach in that costume!"

"Or Ziermann," cried Jan, "or the Goat!" Tommy Thomson retired through the door, deeply offended.

Along the wall opposite the entrance lay three Belgians. The first was called Emile Albert, a well-to-do man, owner of one of the best Brussels cloth businesses and several houses, much traveled and speaking excellent English, German, and French. His left leg had had to be amputated below the knee as soon as he arrived at the hospital. Despite all his money and his beautiful houses, he was a poor man now.

Beside him lay Jacques Piermont, a watchmaker from Bruges, himself as delicate as the works of a lady's watch. Into these sensitive works had flown a shell splinter, destroying the entire mechanism. You had only to look at Jacques to know how things stood with him. His childish face was distorted with pain, his eyes red with tears. He was a God-fearing lad, and when the others made a row and their talk and shouts were criss-crossing the room from corner to corner, he lay with folded hands, praying and praying until the pain tore his prayer apart and his hands clenched on the bed-covers in tortured spasms.

Nurse Veronica went over and gave him another injection. She had to give him one every two hours to make the pain at all bearable. After each injection he could at least sleep for a time.

The third Belgian was called Offenbach. He was a funny dumpling of a man, a Fleming from Beyeren, near Antwerp. Under fire from the German machine guns he had been shot straight through the right collar-bone and was highly delighted. "I've got the classiest wound there is. Every riding gentleman breaks his collarbone sometime, so I'm in aristocratic company!" He was always ready with some clownish comment or other. An artist by trade, he enthusiastically drew everything he saw, especially the black men. He had drawn Jan twice already, sleeping and waking. Now he was in the middle of a portrait of Nurse Veronica. Fleury had promised him three marks for the drawing.

"*Nom d'un chien,*" said Offenbach, "when this filthy business is over I'm going to buy a gypsy caravan and drive all over the world with it painting people cheaply, no matter where they are. Then when they're dead they can go on haunting their children and grandchildren. There's terrific business to be done. No one likes dying, so all you have to say to them is that you're going to 'immortalize' them, and they crawl on the floor and let themselves be 'immortalized' for good money. I'm going to make a sign to put on the front of my little caravan saying: IMMORTALIZATION CENTER. *Ça c'est pas mal, messieurs,* just come right in, folks!" Then the nurse told him to stop his loud chatter, as the little watchmaker gave a terrible groan in his sleep.

Tommy Thomson came in again. He had picked up part of a newspaper on his tour of the school building and wanted to read it. "Anything about peace in there?" asked Cordes. Albert translated the question, but the Scot shook his head and began to undress. His tour had been rather too much for him, and his beautiful uniform had been laughed at in every ward.

"That should happen to every uniform," said Cordes.

"How long is this miserable war going to last, then?" asked the painter.

"How long?" repeated the vineyardist. "Until the Germans have been chased out of our country and my vineyard."

"That means forever," said the bookbinder. "They'll never leave again, not voluntarily at least."

"By force then," replied Fleury. "He who lives by the sword shall die by the sword. The Bible says so."

"What's that supposed to mean?" blazed Voss. "Did *we* start it, eh?"

" 'Oo else?" said Smith, his pipe between clenched teeth. " 'Oo else?"

"Yes, who else?" said the Alsatian eagerly. "You attacked us when we were all at peace."

"Us too," the Belgian agreed.

"We attacked you? That's a joke!" cried the man from Leipzig. "We were attacked, by the Russians, and why? Because they knew quite well you would help them, you French and English!"

"*Pardon*, I didn't want a war," said Fleury.

"Nor me! — Nor me! — *Moi non plus!* — Me neither!" they all shouted at once.

"And I certainly didn't," declared Offenbach. "There's nothing more tedious than drawing uniforms all the time."

"Don't joke, Offenbach!" said Voss angrily. "I'm serious. Do you think I would have gone to war otherwise?"

"*Alors*, why did you go to war?" asked the Alsatian scornfully.

"Why? For the good cause!"

"Good cause is good," said Offenbach.

"Stop joking, Offenbach!" Voss repeated. "I know what I'm fighting for: with God for king and fatherland!"

"God wasn't there when you invaded my poor country," growled Albert.

"That was self-defense," Voss insisted. "When you're attacked — and you attacked us — "

"No, it was you! It was you!" Belgians and Frenchmen cried together. "*We* are fighting in self-defense!"

"No, we are!" the man from Leipzig thundered.

"You surrounded us, that's what you did. I'll tell you exactly why you went to war: out of envy of our industry and jealousy of our splendid fleet."

"Lies!" the Belgian exploded. "We are fighting to free our own country! Who destroyed Louvain and shot down hundreds of innocent civilians? You did!"

"*Liberté, fraternité, égalité!*" muttered a Frenchman feverishly from his corner.

"Do you know what that means?" cried the Brussels householder: "Liberty, fraternity, equality, yes, that's what we and our allies are fighting for, we're fighting for the freedom of the seas and our countries against German barbarism!"

"And alongside the Russian barbarians! You should be ashamed," Voss choked. "We, we are fighting for German civilization, for the holiest possessions of mankind, we alone, with our brothers in Austria and Hungary!"

"Nice brothers you've got there," sneered the Alsatian. "A pretty lot they are, those — "

At that moment the medical corporal, Kaspar Ender, entered the room: "Quiet," he shouted, but none of the fighting cocks took any notice. The Alsatian vine-yardist had made his way up the schoolroom to the bed of the Leipzig bookbinder. Shaking with excitement, he got out: "That Austrian archduke who began the whole filthy business . . . Who knows why he was murdered!"

"And why are we being murdered?" interjected Cordes.

Fleury, paying no attention, said, "If you had told

your 'brothers' to leave the Serbs down there in peace, I would still be sitting in my vineyard, but you were on their side, that wreck of a state, you — "

"That's vile, what you're saying!" stormed Kaspar Ender, the medical orderly. Born twenty-five years before in Vienna, he had taken German nationality at twenty-one, but his heart was still in Vienna. No one was going to insult his Austria. "I'll tell you something," he shouted into the tumult, smashing his fist down on the table in the middle of the room. "We Austrians are fighting for an ideal, if you happen to know what that means, you riffraff! I'm here to tell you that any idiot in Austria knows that, and it's in all our songs, too — "

"What can't be cured must be endured!" Offenbach mocked.

"Hold your tongue!" snapped the corporal. "The way we Austrians feel was made into a song at the very beginning of the war, and I know it by heart:

"*Shall I fall upon the Danube shore,*
Or in Poland will my bones be laid?
It's nought to me
If I can see
Our banners waving over Belgerade!"

"Pretty poem, Corporal," said Lance Corporal Cordes, "I've got nothing against it. Ever been in Belgerade, or Belgrade, Corporal?" Ender shook his head. "Don't expect you'll ever be there, either. Now you tell me honestly, Corporal, what does it matter to you whose flags are flying there? That's for the people of

Belgrade to decide, don't you think? Every country ought to be able to decide for itself what banners are going to wave over it and which ones they feel most at home with."

"*Très bien,*" said the Alsatian approvingly. "We people from Alsace-Lorraine have wanted that for a long time, including the ones on the German side of the frontier, we want to be free — "

"You'd like that, wouldn't you!" Voss objected. "Alsace is German to the core."

"My name is *Fleury,*" the vineyardist retorted, "from *Vernon,* monsieur!"

"Then England ought to start by liberating the Boers," cried Voss, "and the Irish and the Indians and the Egyptians and — "

"And," cried Albert, "you Germans and Austrians should be liberating Poland and the Danes and the Bohemians and — " Oof, the row started all over again. They jumped out of bed in their nightshirts, shouting in every language and dialect until there was such hubbub in the ward that no one could even hear himself speak. All any of them wanted, if they could not convince the rest, was to shout them down.

At last Cordes got on the table and roared: "Quiet! Qui — et! Stop your row, damn it all, have you gone crazy? We're all wounded here, we've all got the same pain, the same fever, and we're going for each other as if we wanted to gobble each other up. Idiots! Ideals? The only ideal is peace. But your ideal is the skull of Sultan Mkwawa, yes, Mkwawa haunts *your* skulls — " But after that no one could hear a word he said as the

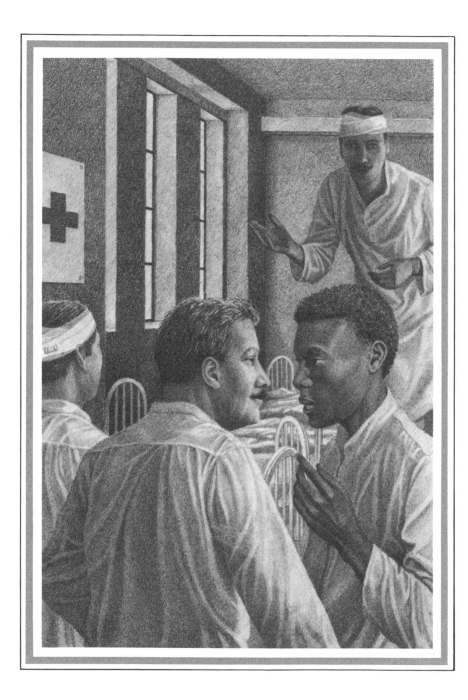

row broke out again, much more violently than before. It came from the black men, who until that point had been looking on, grinning, while the white men fought each other. But suddenly they were completely out of hand. No one could understand them, but from the babble of words one word emerged again and again: Mkwawa, Mkwawa!

Ma-Ka, the fiddler, had slipped out, but now he reappeared with another black man: good God, Jan had seen this man somewhere before. Yes, that was it — the giant who had thrown the hand grenade that had wounded him and Cordes. Heavens, what a giant! He could scarcely get through the door.

Around his massive head was a white bandage from which his frizzy black hair sprouted. A broad scar ran right across his face. Ma-Ka, who looked almost small beside him, waved his hands in the air, babbling like a waterfall: "Sergeant Monsieur Kru-Kru — Sergeant Monsieur Kru-Kru — kss kss — " Incomprehensible, guttural noises came from his mouth as he shook his fist and bared his teeth. His words seemed to be aimed especially at Cordes.

By now more and more black men from the other classrooms had gathered behind them and were pushing Kru-Kru and Ma-Ka slowly forward toward the table on which Cordes — his head bandaged like his opponent's — was still standing. Offenbach, in the corner behind him, was sketching frantically. It was a sinister sight: the dense black mass moving inexorably forward, a sight made all the more grisly by the fact that they were all wounded. They walked with sticks and crutches and flourished them threateningly as they came. Their faces expressed such passionate obsession that the very sight of them inspired terror.

"Get back to your rooms!" ordered Ender. "Left, about face!" They stood like a wall, their eyes fixed on Cordes, who exclaimed: "What do you want from me, you men — *que voulez-vous?*"

Kru-Kru uttered a couple of sentences that seemed to be an answer. Ma-Ka repeated them in French, Emile Albert translated them to the Englishman, and the Alsatian spoke them in German.

"White man," the black sergeant had said, "give us back the sacred skull of our great King Mkwawa! White men robbed our forefathers of it and now white men have promised our chiefs and medicine men that we shall get it back by fighting the Germans."

"What white men?" whispered the Europeans, each in their own languages. "What's this about a skull? Where is it? What does this mean?"

Cordes got down from the table, walked slowly toward the chief, ceremoniously offered him a place on his bed and gestured earnestly to the others to sit down as well. He handed around cigarettes and lit them. Then he spoke, after asking Albert and Ma-Ka to translate accurately everything he said, no matter what it might be: "You black men, I believe everything you have said through the mouth of your Sergeant Kru-Kru. I believe that you have been promised the skull of your Sultan Mkwawa in reward for all the blood that you and your good, brave brothers have poured out on the battlefields of Europe. I have been in Africa myself. I love your country. And I tell you that I and he, my white brother" — he pointed to Voss — "and he and he and he, all of us here have been promised the skull of Sultan Mkwawa in payment for our pain and our blood. They have simply used different names. Instead of saying Mkwawa they said, freedom, fatherland, justice; to some they said, Belgrade; to others, vengeance; to others, Little Father Tsar. Instead of Mkwawa they said: civilization, humanity, or even an honorable peace. But it all meant the same, and out there on the battlefields we have found none of the things we were promised at home: no civilization, no humanity, any more than you, my black brothers, have found the skull of your venerated chief. If I had it — if I had your sacred relic — I would give it to you, but I have only this skull of mine" — his hands went to his head — "though how long I can hang on to it I don't know. I've never seen the skull of your king and I can no more give it to you than you can give me German civilization or the dead Frenchman his vengeance or these captured Englishmen the freedom of the sea or Ender there his banners over Belgrade or Emile Albert with his amputated leg the neutrality of Belgium. All of us, black and white, were dragged into the war for an illusion, each of us for a different one, but all those mirages have dissolved in the mists of blood on the battlefields. Monsieur Sergeant Kru-Kru, Monsieur Ma-Ka, give me your hand — "

At that moment the little watchmaker, Jacques Piermont from Bruges, with the baby face, sat straight up in bed, his fever-glazed eyes transfigured with a strange fire, glared at the circle of black and white men, and said in a clear, childish voice: "The peace of God be with you all. Amen."

Then he sank back and died. All the men who had been so loud in their anger against each other so short a time before stood around the dead man and were silent.

❖ SIT DOWN, KUBITZKY!

WHILE ALL THIS WAS GOING ON IN FIELD Hospital XXXIV A, the Supreme Commander of the German Army was sitting in the great study of his general headquarters a few miles behind the front. He was sitting in a leather armchair with a high, carved back and armrests that ended in lions' heads, for the supreme commander wanted everything he saw to be expressive of victory. Victory and empire. The lion he regarded as the finest symbol, for the lion is the king of the desert.

The whole room was filled with royal animals and symbols of victory: the king of the air, an eagle wrought in metal, was enthroned on the edge of an ashtray. The king of cunning, a snake, carved in wood, carried his desk lamp. The legs of his desk were polished vultures. A bearskin, complete with head, hung on one wall. His pencil ended in a crown, there was a crown on every cigarette, specially manufactured for the supreme commander. They were quite a bit longer than the cigarettes of ordinary mortals.

A corpulent elderly man in a black coat stood humbly beside the emperor. In his hand he held a leather briefcase containing folders and in the folders there were documents. Written on one of the folders was: "Subject: Petition on behalf of the Polish boy Jan Kubitzky" and inside it was the application written by Allenstetten in the train on Christmas Eve and a pile of other papers, all relating to Jan. Each of the many offices through which the application had passed in the last three months had had a finger in the pie and the cardboard folder was by now swollen with paper words — but that was only the beginning, there was more to come.

Scarcely had the swollen folder passed through the supreme commander's study when such activity was set in train that you would have thought that the outcome of the whole war and the fortunes of mankind depended on that sheaf of paper. There was telegraphing and telephoning, conversations in which meetings were called and canceled; orders were given, each one longer than the last, and the further down the orders penetrated, the longer they grew. Only Jan, the subject of it all, had not an inkling.

The German, French, and Belgian death factories at the front were in full operation again. Room had constantly to be made in the field hospitals for new transports of wounded.

Black men and white, Alsatians and Scots, Walloons and Flemings, *poilu* and Tommy, the Briton with the German grandparents and the Belgian with the German name, all had to go. Some were hobbling on sticks and crutches, others lying on stretchers. Anyone without German nationality was sent to a prisoner-of-war camp or hospital.

The fine days of Neuville were over, for fine they had been, despite pain and fever, despite the stench and the din. The sixteen men left in the big blue schoolroom had been through quite a lot. Something new had entered into their lives that would never be completely lost.

When Jan, his arm still bandaged, stepped out into the street for the first time, it had just been raining. In the sky were white clouds through which the sun was now shining again. The air had a silvery shimmer that was reflected everywhere: on the wet red roofs, the soaked pavements, the fresh green of the trees, and the forest of weeds that had shot up in the school garden.

Opposite the school building a narrow alley led to a stream where laundry was washed and on the other side stood tall poplars and birches, like the ones at home by the Ravka. There was a bridge across it, too, and a jetty like the one in Kopchovka, and over the poplars, the birches, the river, and the bridge, lay the same delicate, silvery haze, into which Jan entered as in a dream. All about him was peace.

But a dull growling and rumbling, a deep, persistent thunder pierced his dream, awakening him and warning him: don't count on peace! He would so much have liked to count on it, to have run across the bridge and through the burgeoning meadows with Flox at his side. . . .

But Flox was not there — where could he be now? Was he still in that dark dugout under the narrow trench, poor creature, accustomed as he was to freedom, light, air, and his own master, none of which were his now?

In the former teachers' room, which now served as the hospital office, Jan found that the Seventh Battery was still in its old position. The battery quarters were not very far from the hospital, and Jan was shown the way. There had also been a message from the battery commander telling Jan to return at once, as soon as his health was restored. He would be told why when he got there. Voss and Cordes were being sent on leave to convalesce.

"Good luck, Cordes!"

"Good luck, Panie, and say hello to them all. Look after that arm! Hello to Flox, too!"

The Seventh was quartered about an hour beyond the trench where the guns were mounted and was easy to find. The thunder of the front, which grew louder as he advanced, told him the direction, and soon he reached a village at the foot of a vineyard slope on top of which stood a fine old country house, surrounded by huge, blooming magnolia trees. The little village had about a hundred houses, of which more than half had been destroyed. This was the battery's relief position.

In front of a stable where the village began he found Drivers Müller, Uhl, and the pockmarked Podlesch peeling potatoes for the field kitchen. Jan's arrival astonished them. "Can't you ever get enough?" said

Müller. "The air's pretty thick again up there. You can hear the guns." Jan could hear them. "Is Flox still up there?" he asked. They shrugged their shoulders. "Better ask the orderly room fellows," said Uhl.

The orderly room was close by and the "fellows" were Corporal Schulz, who suffered from stomach upset for which he took large quantities of a white powder, and the militiaman Micke, a sly, cheerful little fellow, a beekeeper by trade.

"Hurrah, there he is, the national hero!" cried Schulz, spilling his bismuth powder, which he was just lifting to his mouth on the end of a knife. "You're to report at once to our sergeant and then to the battery commander, pronto!"

"Where is Lance Corporal Poodle?" asked Jan.

"Oh, Lord, he can't move anymore at all," said Micke. "Spends his whole time underneath the supply wagon," pointing out of the window, "right along the street, then left. But before that, you go to the second house on the right, the one with the railing, and report yourself!" Jan didn't give it a thought.

He was thinking only of Flox, and he flew down the street to the parking area, where the dog was lying on a bundle of straw under the supply wagon. When he recognized Jan he tried to wag his tail, but he was a pitiful sight. His nose was hot, his eyes dim, his coat befouled and bloody. A wound was festering on his left hind leg. He looked bad.

Ziermann, the lathe-operator, and Schlenska, the mechanic, came over from the blacksmith's wagon to greet Jan.

"Poor old dog," said Ziermann. "Won't eat at all, won't drink at all. I think he's going."

"What have you done to him?" Jan yelled at him in despair.

"Us? Nothing at all," Ziermann objected, and Schlenska put in, "I'd just like to know what we've got vets in this place for! Call themselves veterinary officers — they don't give a damn for a poor animal like that."

"I've looked after the little dog myself," Ziermann apologized. "When you went off on watch, you've no idea, there was no doing anything with him. And any time I went out, he was right on my tail — what was I to do? One, two, three — he was gone! He's got a will of his own, that one, he looked everywhere for you. Then when the shooting started, he didn't get far. The guard that relieved me heard him barking and howling and whining and brought him in. We got the bullet out and brought him here. It's better than the dugout. The rats would have eaten him long since."

"Flox, poor Floxy, what am I to do with you?" moaned Jan.

"I've never seen the like," said Schlenska. "Three staff vets, but doctor an animal like this one — no, no question!"

"Are the vets a long way from here?" asked Jan quickly.

"Fifteen, maximum twenty minutes," said Schlenska. "That big house up there behind the magnolias."

Jan clasped Flox under his right arm — the left was

still bandaged. The dog rested his muzzle on Jan's shoulder and off they went.

Veterinary Captain Reppich and his two colleagues were leading an extremely comfortable life in the attractive country house. They were bursting with health, and their work was pleasant. While the death factory went on working up ahead, they were having their orderlies make boxes for them in a barn. Each box had sixty neat compartments lined with wood shavings and cotton wool. Each box was a roost for sixty hens. Those vets had organized a splendid bit of poultry farming for themselves, not on behalf of sick soldiers to whom an occasional egg might have been very helpful, but exclusively for their own private use. They fed the hens on fodder intended for the horses because, so Captain Reppich said, the horses always had enough to eat and it would do no harm if his chickens took a share. But in the midst of his peaceful activity his talk was always warlike. If a trench was lost at the front or a hill was not held, he talked of quitters in need of a good deal more discipline. But boxes of eggs were sent to his wife, who liked egg custards and cakes made with eggs. He sent plenty of meat home, too, for Mrs. Reppich liked meat.

In Germany at that time both meat and eggs were a great rarity. Most families had neither.

When Jan arrived with Flox, Reppich was most indignant. "I've got something better to do than treat mongrels," he snapped, but Jan begged and pleaded.

"Please, Captain, sir, please help. What am I to do with him, what should I do?"

"As far as I'm concerned, put him down by the wall there," said the vet graciously, "and be off!" And to one of the orderlies busy with eggboxes he snapped, "Get my pistol from the chest in the hall." As the orderly ran into the house, Reppich spat at the others: "It's a disgrace, the way you treat those eggs, you blockheads! Another two cracked — you only do it so that you can eat them yourselves. I'll put a spoke in your wheels, I'll send you to the trenches, that will make you think. If one more of you breaks an egg, you'll all be sent away, understand?"

Jan still had not understood what Reppich intended. His heart stood still when the man walked over to the wall where the poor creature lay, drew his pistol from its leather holster, raised it and took aim — in one leap Jan was beside Flox and threw himself across the dog.

"My God, what in thunder?" shouted Reppich in a fright. "I might have shot you, you damned bumpkin. Be off with you!"

As fast as he had reached the wall, Jan was gone, but now Flox was in his arms and he was running through the back gate like the wind and, through the vines and across the fields, without looking back. Then he and the dog huddled down in a small depression. Flox did not stir.

What shall I do now? Oh, what shall I do? kept going through Jan's head. Oh, if only Vladimir were here, nothing like this would have happened. How he used to

take care of those sheep, how he looked after them
when anything was wrong! He knew what to do for
every ailment: herbs, salves, compresses — if he could
see his Flox in this condition, oh he would . . . yes, what
would he do? What would Vladimir have done for
poor, sick Flox? Jan thought and thought: What had
Vladimir done that time with the little billy goat when
it got mixed up with the strange herd and was bitten by
the wolfhound? Hadn't he used earth or clay or something? Perhaps, if he put some earth on Flox's wound
now . . . or clay? There was a lot of that here. Would
that help?

Jan pulled out the pocketknife that Papa had given
him and dug it into the clay. The shepherd had done
that, too, he remembered now; he'd made the clay wet,
stirred it up into a little paste, and then smeared it on
the wound.

He got water from the ditch behind the alders. He had
a handkerchief, too, and he smeared some of the paste
on it, laid it carefully on the wound, then bound the
whole thing firmly with the sling that had held his arm.

What did his arm need a sling for! If only Flox would
get better again.

In the meantime, there was a terrible row going on in
the orderly room of the Seventh. Naturally because of
Jan, who had made off. "Nothing but trouble, that boy.
High time he became a proper soldier," fumed Sergeant Dietrich. "Then he'll learn a thing or two! Because of his unpunctuality, I get called on the carpet.
Why didn't you send him straight to me?"

"I did tell him, Sergeant — I pointed out your quarters to him," Micke said defensively.

"You should have come with him."

"Beg pardon, sir. I thought — "

"A soldier's not supposed to think," broke in Dietrich and strode angrily across the office. "What on earth is he up to now?"

"He didn't tell me, Sarge," said Micke.

"You must have some idea. *Think!*"

"You just told me not to think, Sarge," said Micke, his face expressionless.

"Don't you try any of your jokes on me, or I'll get nasty! You'll go and find the boy at once, and hurry up about it. The lieutenant is in a filthy temper."

Turning correctly on his heel, Micke left the room, but once outside his steps slowed. He decided to do the job thoroughly. He asked questions at every house and stopped to speak to every man he met. At last he bumped into Ziermann, who sent him up to the house, and Reppich, where Micke first lingered to have the brilliant invention of the eggboxes explained to him by the orderlies. "Well, at least we know now where all the good things we don't get are going." He nodded understandingly. Then the captain arrived and threw him out. As luck would have it, by the front entrance, so that Micke was able to waste another three hours wandering around among the trellised vines before he found Jan in his hollow.

Jan was still sitting with Flox, renewing the dressing for the fourth time. The patient seemed in a better state already, his earnest dog's eyes gazing thankfully at his young doctor.

However hard Micke pressed him, Jan would not leave his dog. "Jan, be reasonable," pleaded Micke, "I'm going to be in big trouble. The lieutenant is in a bad temper to start with. He's sprained his foot and can't move, so he swears for exercise and we're bearing the brunt of it in the office. Do it for me, Panie! I'll stay with your dog. You can trust me, I'm a beekeeper."

Jan gave in at last. "But pay attention!" he insisted. "When the compress is dry, put on a fresh one at once!"

"I will, I will, I'll treat the leg as if it were my own, count on me!" promised Micke. "But you go to Allenstetten right away, promise me."

"Stir the clay thoroughly," Jan was still shouting from a distance. "No little lumps. They hurt!"

In spite of his sprained foot, Allenstetten greeted Jan with the greatest friendliness. Not a word of reproach for his lateness, and he even offered the boy a cigarette, which Jan refused. "Sit down, Kubitzky," he said. What's going on? Jan wondered.

"My dear Kubitzky," began the battery commander, "you're not a boy anymore. You've proved yourself a hero, yes, a hero! It's time for your heroic deeds in the Eastern theater of war to earn their due reward. Will you have a drink?" Jan refused again and the officer continued, "As commander of the company you voluntarily selected, I have at last, after great efforts, at last succeeded in getting your naturalization papers through."

"Is that how you sprained your foot?" asked Jan. Allenstetten looked surprised. "What? How? Oh, I see, you don't know what naturalization means. Well, it means that you're to become a German, like your comrades. The application has gone all the way up to supreme headquarters, and I think I have good reason to assume that even the supreme commander himself has taken a lively interest in you. I just wanted to tell you. I think you will know what to make of that high honor!"

During this speech Jan had been thinking of nothing but the moist compresses: it might be a good thing to make one for the lieutenant's sprained foot as well. That would make more sense than all this talk.

Allenstetten went on: "You will appear to your new fatherland as a shining example of inspired devotion and true sacrificial courage. Remembering the boy hero of Kopchovka, both old and young will flock to the standard with renewed enthusiasm. Your example should be particularly effective in the success of the war loan — carrying on a war is a matter of money, money, and more money, and the poorest of the poor will joyfully give their last mite for the cause. Above all, however, I would like you to know that there is a rumor in the highest circles that after the expected complete conquest of your Polish homeland, the youth of Poland will follow your example and establish a voluntary army of their own within the German Army. Then Polish troops will march to victory side by side with the Germans. The thought of you will give them courage and enthusiasm. Sergeant Dietrich will tell you the rest. You may go."

❖ VOLUNTEERS FOR FOOD TRANSPORT!

NO COMPRESSES COULD HELP HIM, THOUGHT Jan, leaving Allenstetten's office. He must have sprained his brain box as well: boy hero, heroic deeds, courage, money, fatherland, sergeant, war loan, it was enough to drive a person mad. But one thing I do see: they need a new Mkwawa, they simply want to make a Mkwawa out of me, as if there weren't enough men running into the machine guns already! They should damn well leave me in peace. I'm hungry, and so is Flox.

To the field kitchen!

But the new cook did not know him. He came from the reserve hospital a long way off and had only been with the battery for three days. "Panie?" he grunted when Jan introduced himself. "Nothing like that here. Better get back to Russia — you'll find as many panies as you want there. You'll get nothing from me, hands off!"

"Where are the others, then? They'll give me something," Jan objected, standing firm.

"Don't talk so dumb! They'll give you something indeed! They've got nothing themselves, they're up front. Front! Haven't you heard the guns all day? It's been going on for more than twenty hours now. They've had nothing to eat since ten last night."

"Then why doesn't someone take them something?" asked Jan.

"Stupid talk! There's a barrage being laid down between us and them, no one can get through alive."

"But someone must get through and get food to them," said Jan.

"Someone? At least four," said the cook. "If it doesn't stop soon I'll load one of these boilers on my back and go myself. Whether I get there is another question."

"I'll go with you. Hang on a minute, I've got something to see to," said Jan.

The cook stared at him: "Not yet dry behind the ears and you want to go through a barrage? With a boiler full of food? Have you any idea? You're just trying to wheedle something out of me. Oh, well, there's some pea soup you can have."

"Thanks," said Jan, beginning to spoon it down. "Can I take those bones with me?" he asked, pointing to the floor.

"Them old bones? Whatever for?"

"For my dog," said Jan, gathering up the scattered remains and running back with them to the clay hollow where Flox and Micke were anxiously awaiting him.

The poodle was greedy for his meal, his strength already returning.

"You take a good lump of clay with you so you can

go on looking after the dog in your billet!" Micke advised him. "You take the dog, I'll take the clay."

It was good advice. Laden with clay and poodle, the two walked back to the orderly room. The fearful barrage that was cutting off the crews of the Seventh Battery from billets and food was still unbroken. Jan seemed to see their hollow-eyed faces before him: Mustard's nose jutting more bonily than ever from his narrow face, Hottenrot, his mouth hanging open, Dambach chewing the stem of his empty pipe, their stomachs grumbling — and all the time they had to drag up shells, shoot, and be shot at — it was ghastly. Jan glanced at his watch: another hour and a half had passed and still the guns went on.

Micke had made Flox comfortable on a horse blanket in the little room behind the orderly room and promised Jan that he would take good care of him. "You can have my supper, too. But then, straight to the sergeant!" he said, pushing him out of the door. "Second house on the right, with the railings."

"Why do I have to go again?" asked Jan unwillingly.

"How should I know? Hero lessons!" said Micke brightly. "They want to make a national monument out of you or something. They're going to photograph you and paint you, and I think you'll have to make a speech."

"What's all this for?" asked Jan, giving Micke an angry look.

"Well, I can't do anything about it," said Micke. "No one is lending me anything for my beekeeping, but for the war, the damned war, they'll throw away millions.

They'll use you for that. Your picture will be stuck up on all the walls with a notice saying: Subscribe to war loans!"

"Bosh," said Jan and walked off to the field kitchen where the cook was distributing the rations for supper. Fat 125 grams, cheese 125 grams — but there were scarcely twenty men waiting in line. All the others were up at the front, victims of hunger and the guns. The twenty stood there with long, frightened faces, listening to the dull, distant growling that never stopped.

"This is no good," said the cook. "We can't just let them croak up there. Who's coming? Here are the boilers with their dinners. I need five men. Who's coming?" He waited. When no one volunteered: "Right then, I'll be the first. Got a spot of heart trouble, but I'm going. Who else?"

"Volunteers for suicide," muttered Uhl.

"What are you getting out of your life, then? The war — this isn't living!" said Driver Müller, and he too volunteered. Podlesch stepped forward beside him. He had a tendency to melancholy anyway. "You're quite right, I've had enough, too."

"But we need two more," said the cook and waited. "The way you all shout 'Here!' The way you all push and shove!" he mocked.

Then Jan came in from the office, saw the three men by the full food boilers and joined them.

"This is our good angel!" cried Hannes Ziermann. "If he's coming, nothing can go wrong," and he lifted a boiler straight away. "Gawd, is that a weight!"

"Panie," said Micke in the office, "remember, you've got to see the sergeant first."

"There's plenty of time for that," said Jan. "There's not plenty of time for them," and he pointed at the lidded boilers. Then they set off.

As they reached the end of the village Ziermann, who had not left Jan's side, said, "If I do happen to get it, I've got me epitaph ready, wrote it meself:

"Ziermann, who in this grave is lying,
Spent his life in turning iron.
The iron turned against him then
And blew him from the life of men.

"Nice, ain't it? You've got to write that on me gravestone. Think you can remember it?"

"Gravestone! You're a great loony," grumbled Müller. "You'll be lucky if you end up in a mass grave."

With every step the five were approaching the ghastly barrage. With every step the roar intensified. The shells cracked, the shrapnel exploded more and more menacingly. How could a man get through — and with the heavy boilers that hindered every movement!

Now they were in the midst of it, flinging themselves into trenches, clambering up again, seeking shelter from the hail of shot, falling into shell holes, climbing out, sliding into ditches —

Behind and ahead of them the whole air was black with the earth spurting up in thick clumps under the impact of the shells. How could a man get through?

Podlesch gave a cry, dropped his boiler, threw up his arms, and fell.

Death had found Gottfried Podlesch. His boiler rolled over the edge of a trench. A moment later Müller too cried out, wounded in one arm. The lathe-operator tugged his field dressing from his tunic and bandaged him. Then they helped him into an old, shell-struck dugout.

On! On!

The cook with the weak heart was finished. "No good," he gasped from a shell hole. "Leave me here!"

Now only Jan and Ziermann were left. Ziermann repeated over and over to himself: "My good angel, my good angel, don't desert me!" Jan was praying: "Don't let anything happen to Ziermann, dear God, I can't get the boilers there alone." His arm had started to ache again.

They pulled planks from a trench and tied the four boilers on them with straps and braces, like a kind of sledge. They harnessed themselves to it and pulled, flinging themselves into the next shell hole whenever they heard a shot howling toward them.

Go on, only go on! There could not be more than six minutes to go.

But that six minutes turned into almost three-quarters of an hour. We're not going to make it, I'm not going to make it. . . .

But they made it. Slowly, slowly, the rain of fire was left behind: there was the trench. There was the battery!

Their comrades ran toward them, tore the boilers open, and ate and ate, smacking their lips and repeating with full mouths: "You're our good angel, you're the best fellow in the world, you too, Ziermann, we'll never forget this, none of us — "

❖ THE GREAT DAY

HAT WAS ON SUNDAY. ON MONDAY THE BAT-
tery was withdrawn from the firing line. They
owed that to Jan. The great day on which he
was to be turned into a German Maid of Orleans was at
hand. Only the final preparations had still to be made.

On Thursday Sergeant Dietrich read out the following Battery Order to the men assembled south of the
village:

Tomorrow our Supreme Commander will honor the
Seventh Battery with a visit.

The battery will parade at 9 A.M. in full marching
order on the park, officers on the right wing, then non-
commissioned officers and men.

In view of this supreme distinction awarded to the
battery for its services on behalf of our beloved father-
land, I expect everyone to behave in a manner befitting
an occasion of such importance and in particular all
uniforms to be in immaculate condition.

For this purpose there will be a full parade at 6 P.M.
today in marching order. Any items missing or ren-

dered unsightly will be borrowed from other units on the orders of the High Command. The quartermaster sergeant will submit a list of items to be obtained to me at the beginning of the parade.

Between 7 and 10 today, during cleaning time, further detailed instructions will be given. Special importance will be attached to the men's ability to give a brief and specific reply to any questions that may be addressed to them. I refer you in particular to the following questions that are certain to be asked:

What is your name?

What is your occupation?

How long have you served?

Have you any children?

What are their names?

How long have you been on the western front?

Where were you in the East?

If the Kaiser should ask: "Do you want to go home?" you will answer: "Very good, Your Majesty, but not until we've won."

To the question: "How do you like it?" the reply will be: "As any German soldier would."

His Majesty must leave us in the certainty that there can be only one outcome to this war: victory!

As soon as His Majesty leaves his car, the battery will give three cheers. Lieutenant Ruschatzky will practice the cheers with the men for half an hour before today's afternoon parade. The right hand will remain on the carbine strap above the cartridge pouch, the left hand down the left trouser seam.

When the salute is taken, on the command: "Eyes —

right!" the head will be turned in the direction indicated to look at His Majesty. The man will follow His Majesty with his eyes, turning his head as far as the third man on his right, and will then return to the "eyes front" position without further orders.

Comrades, I expect you all to join in making this day of honor for the battery into an incomparable occasion.

VON ALLENSTETTEN, BATTERY COMMANDER

Postscript: Jan Kubitzky, until now a Russian but from tomorrow onwards a German national, will stand on the left wing, three paces distant from the left flank man. He will wear the field uniform appointed by the High Command, with side arms but without carbine. Lieutenant Ruschatzky will instruct him in every detail once again this evening during the general cleaning, mending, and instruction time, since it is expected that His Majesty will have a lengthier conversation with Kubitzky.

After tomorrow the form of address employing the foreign term Panie used for Kubitzky will cease. From now on our comrade will be addressed by his proper name.

Jan's new uniform was already laid out in his billet in the village fire station that had been allotted to the third and fourth gun crews. Flox was sitting in front of it, on guard. His leg was healing, his eyes bright, his coat freshly washed for the day's celebrations.

Jan's eyes were troubled. He changed from the old

uniform into the new as if in a dream. "Subscribe to war loans!" he murmured to himself at one point.

"Hold your tongue, Panie — oh, pardon," cried Mustard, "I meant shut your supremely majestic yap, Lord High-muckety-muck! What are we to subscribe to war loans with? They must have got your brains!"

"I didn't mean you, Mustard, don't be such a donkey," said Jan. "I was thinking of Rosenlöcher. He was going to sell his garden for the war loan."

Then he went off to Ru for hero's class while the others went to polish-and-mend.

"Sit down, Kubitzky," said Ru, when Jan came in. "Do you remember that time when we unmasked the spy together? Wasn't that fine?"

"Mmm," said Jan.

"Memories are always fine," said the teacher, "but now let's think of the future, Jan, because there's something great and fine ahead of you. Do you remember, in that little farm cottage where I left my map case, how you told me what you wanted to be? A bridge builder, you said. Well, Kubitzky, from tomorrow on you're going to be called upon to help build another bridge, the bridge to victory!"

"I'd rather build a real bridge, like the one in Cologne," said Jan.

"After a victorious peace, of course," said the professor, "and you will be playing your part in that. Do you know the story of the Maid of Orleans?"

"No," said Jan.

Ru frowned and went on, "Well, the Maid of Orleans grew up in the country like you and her name was

Jeanne, very like yours, Jan, and she inspired her fellow-countrymen so much that they chased the enemy out of their country."

"How am I supposed to chase the Germans out of Poland?" asked Jan.

"But Jan," said Ru, "who mentioned anything like that? The Germans and Poles are friends now. We're talking about the enemies of Germany."

"What enemies are we supposed to be chasing out of Germany then? There aren't any in it," said Jan.

"I didn't mean that," said Ru, who was gradually losing patience. "We have to defeat the enemy in his own country, otherwise he will come into our country and then, woe betide us all! Woe to the defeated!"

"Do you know the story of Sultan Mkwawa?" asked Jan thoughtfully.

"You're being very inattentive today," said his teacher crossly, "what do your silly African tales matter to me? If you want something to read, you can come and ask me from time to time. I'll be glad to give you a good book, if you like."

"Yes, sir," said Jan, "but there is a book, someone told me about it in Gradicz, and it says: *no man must.* I'd like to read that book. Have you got it?"

"Aha, *Nathan the Wise*," said the schoolmaster. "There's plenty of time for that. That's for the senior classes. The main thing now is that you should do yourself credit tomorrow. I've made a list here of all the skirmishes and battles in which you have taken part, with the dates. You're to learn that by heart for me by tomorrow morning. If it's too much for you, just learn

the ones underlined in red. You'll report to me at half-
past eight and I'll hear them quickly for you."

Jan pocketed the paper and went first to pick up his
rations, then to his billet, where he collected his kit bag.
When he was at the door Dambach called, "Want to
leave us, do you? Rather be with the officers now?
We're not refined enough for you now, eh?"

"Don't be so disgusting!" cried Jan.

"Where are you off to with that kit bag?" asked Distelmann.

"I've got something to do," said the boy.

"Aha, another deed of heroism," said Mustard,
yawning.

"Maybe," said Jan, gently scratching Flox, who was
looking up at his master. Then he left the billet.

"No one is going to make a Mkwawa of us, Flox," he
said, as they crossed the village square. "*No man must,*
and that means you and me, too." Flox pushed his
muzzle into Jan's hand and they disappeared into the
darkness.

The next morning the Seventh Battery was paraded
on the parking lot at full strength and in full marching
order as never before. As befitted such a significant occasion, all their uniforms were in immaculate condition.

Alert was present with his entire staff, including a
few officers from the Eighth Battery, Captain Jürgensen of the Medical Corps, and Veterinary Captain Reppich with his two colleagues, as well as representatives
of many newspapers, the war correspondents, a bunch
of amiable and contented men. Photographers and cam-

eramen, war artists with their sketchbooks — all were
there. A detachment of cavalry barred the entrances so
that no unauthorized person might slip in and jeopard-
ize the life of His Imperial Majesty the Supreme Commander.

Only the two main participants were missing, and it
was already ten minutes to nine. "That's what they call
military punctuality," whispered one witty war correspondent. Sergeant Dietrich ran through the village,
sweating and swearing, while the two orderlies
careered through fields and vineyards at his orders.
"You'll get him here, the rascal, even if you've got to
drag him here by the hair," the sergeant told them.

At twenty-five to ten Micke returned. He had found
something in a clay pit behind the veterinary officers'
quarters and had brought it to show his officers. It was
a uniform, which the quartermaster sergeant who was
called in recognized as the one allocated to Jan Kubitzky by the High Command — full field uniform
with sidearms.

Von Allenstetten was flabbergasted. This *would*
happen to him, with the supreme commander arriving
at any minute!

The officers put their heads together. What a stupid
business! What could it mean? The whole thing was
quite unthinkable!

"How can one know," said the White Raven, "what
was going on in the boy's head? All of us are so convinced that there is no greater honor on earth, but is
that really true? Is it really such an honor to become a
soldier and a German?"

Quivering with indignation, Allenstetten interrupted: "Excuse me, Captain, I don't think that point of
view is quite correct. I find Kubitzky's conduct absolutely scandalous. The lout deserves a thrashing."

"I must ask you not to use those expressions, Lieutenant," Alert retorted sharply. "Without that boy you
would probably not be here today, nor would I, for that
matter."

"And yet I explained to him last night what this
honor meant!" moaned Ru.

"That doesn't mean he necessarily agreed with you,"
said Alert. "Who knows what his reasons may be."

"Rubbish, reasons!" Reppich intervened. "A common or garden deserter! I'd just like to — "

"Why don't you send me a couple of cases of eggs for
my men, Captain!" said Alert, and turning his back on
the astonished vet, he went over to Jürgensen, who had
been watching the excited scene with great serenity.
"Laughable: a deserter!" he said. "The boy is not yet
fifteen years old and there's no need for him to be a soldier at all. Do you know, my dear Alert, quite frankly,
of all the things the boy has done up to now, this disap-
pearance appeals to me most of all: not a single soldier
has yet bolted from too great an honor; you need the
kind of pluck our Panie's got for that. At least we can
call him Panie again now!"

"How about dismissing the men, Lieutenant?" asked
Alert.

"Yes, but what about His Majesty. We'll wait for
His Majesty, won't we, Captain?"

"It's almost ten now," said Alert with a smile. "According to the latest reports, the neighboring areas will be busy with a major push from the other side by midday. Naturally, they know all about it at headquarters, and in the circumstances I would be surprised if we could expect a visit from our supreme commander now. I'm only wondering why we haven't heard about the cancellation yet. . . . Perhaps you'd better check it again by telephone."

"Battery, dismiss!" ordered von Allenstetten, and Rosshorn, the war correspondent, said, "I've never seen such a comic performance of *Joan of Arc* before."

The gun crews of the Seventh Battery were free for the rest of the day, but they were not happy. Their Panie had gone.

"He'll never come back again," Hannes Ziermann lamented, "he's gone. I'd give me other earlobe, I'd give an arm to have the boy back. Our good angel! Things would have been so great for him now — whyever did he do it?"

Then Father Distelmann stood up, looked around the circle of his friends, and spoke slowly, "I knew him from the very beginning, isn't that right, Hottenrot, when we were advancing near Lodz. He always showed us the right way, always the right way. . . . I believe he's done the same thing this time."

"Us? The right way?" asked Hottenrot.

"Not only us, them over there, too, the *poilus* and the Tommies . . . everyone, the whole world."

"I don't get it," said Hottenrot, pulling off his uniform.

❖ AFTERWORD

J AN KUBITZKY, KNOWN AS PANIE, HAD GONE AND did not come back.
   Gunner Senf, known as Mustard, wrote to Cordes, and Father Distelmann wrote to Albin Rosenlöcher. Neither of them knew anything, not even Papa. Papa wrote to his niece, Elizabeth, known as Sissi, but she had heard nothing of the boy either.

Hans Alert, known as the White Raven, wrote to Aerial Observer Heinz Wolfart, who asked his school friend Eugen Papke — all in vain.

Even in Kopchovka information was requested. Ostrovsky, the missing landowner, had returned, but he knew nothing of any Jan Kubitzky. How was he to know the name of every boy he had thrashed at one time or another?

Nobody knows where Jan went and whether or not he is still alive.

Perhaps this book, which gives an account of Jan and his thoughts and deeds, may happen to fall into the hands of someone who will be reminded that he knew a man to whom these things happened in the years

1914–15 in the East and in the West. Perhaps in this way we shall learn something more of Jan.

Like Jan Kubitzky, the skull of Sultan Mkwawa has failed to return, to this very day. It was mentioned only once again, in 1919, in the Peace Treaty of Versailles, signed at the end of four years of world war.

Article 246 of the Treaty reads as follows:

WITHIN SIX MONTHS FROM THE COMING INTO FORCE OF THE PRESENT TREATY, . . . GERMANY WILL HAND OVER TO HIS BRITANNIC MAJESTY'S GOVERNMENT THE SKULL OF THE SULTAN MKWAWA WHICH WAS REMOVED FROM THE PROTECTORATE OF GERMAN EAST AFRICA AND TAKEN TO GERMANY.

But even this has failed to bring the sacred relic of Africa to light.